UE
University of East Anglia

Creative Writing Anthologies

2013

UEA Prose Fiction Anthology 2013

First published by Egg Box Publishing 2013

International © 2013 retained by individual authors

A CIP record for this book is available from the British Library.

UEA Prose Fiction Anthology 2013 is typeset in 10pt Caslon with 13pt leading. Titles in Din, of various weights.

Printed and bound in the UK by Imprint Digital.

Designed and typeset by Sean Purdy.

Cover photography by Christopher Corby.

Proofread by Sarah Gooderson.

Distributed by Central Books.

ISBN: 9780957661103

Acknowledgements

··

Thanks are due to the School of Literature, Drama and Creative Writing at UEA in partnership with Egg Box Publishing for making this anthology possible.

We'd also like to thank the following people:

Moniza Alvi, Amit Chaudhuri, Andrew Cowan, William Fiennes, Giles Foden, Sarah Gooderson, Lavinia Greenlaw, Rachel Hore, Kathryn Hughes, Katie Konyn, Daniel Leeson, Michael Lengsfield, Jean McNeil, Natalie Mitchell, Beatrice Poubeau, Rob Ritchie, Michèle Roberts, James Scudamore, Ali Smith, Helen Smith, Henry Sutton, George Szirtes, Val Taylor, Steve Waters and Peter Womack.

Nathan Hamilton at Egg Box Publishing and Sean Purdy.

Editorial team:

Beatrice Armstrong
Krishan Coupland
Timothy Lawrence
Rachel Mendel
Matthew McGuinness
Faith Ng
Caroline Pearce
Lauren Rose
Naomi Spicer
Jo Surzyn
Laura Westerman

Contents

....

....

....

Foreword

Joe Dunthorne

When I first visited UEA, for an undergraduate open day, our student guide couldn't help but name-drop alumni of the creative writing course. As we walked the concrete walkways, it was not hard to imagine where Ian McEwan got the title for *The Cement Garden*. At closing time in the union bar, it was easy to think of Kazuo Ishiguro contemplating the unreliability of memory. When I was an undergraduate, we imagined that everyone on the MA was a Man Booker Prize winner-in-waiting. We talked about the course as though it were the end point of a prospective writing career, or rather the point at which we would no longer have to try.

When I started on the MA myself, the quality of the first stories we workshopped seemed to confirm this. They had potential. That was before I realised that everyone was handing in the stories they'd spent the previous five years perfecting. By the end of the first term, the showboating was over and we were submitting work of which we were thoroughly ashamed. This seemed an important moment. Once we'd established nobody was a genius, we could get started on the important business of failing.

I had also expected that MA-level feedback would be more unified. The opposite was true. As an undergraduate, I could at least be corrected on definite things. I remember being taught how to split a line of dialogue with a speech tag and physical description so that characters walked and talked, rather than walked then talked. But by the time I reached the MA, all the simple, solid lessons had been used up and we were faced with the painful task of having our own opinions. When I got back the twelve annotated copies of my stories, I invariably turned to what I thought were my best lines to see how they had fared. The bad news was that nobody agreed on anything or, worse, made no comment at all. How could it be they had nothing to say about such a powerful simile? I could only assume they had accidentally turned two pages at once.

Over the year, we all found people whose perspectives we valued and, for many of us, those people are still our first readers. The MA gave us space, support, and time enough to realise that a year was not nearly enough time. Just last month, I was sent the proofs of a novel – Martin Bannister's debut *A Map of Nowhere* – of which I had read the first chapters in a workshop nearly ten years ago.

As the year wore on, it became increasingly clear that the MA was not going to supply the other thing we had all been promised: bountiful sexual intrigue. I had been told we would drink and yell and cry and hate each other, fall in love and cross boundaries too numerous to mention. Then, in the stories we handed in, our characters would drink, yell, cry, hate and love in thinly disguised romans à clef. As far as I remember – and I'm happy to be corrected – this never happened. It was a year of lowered expectations.

All those reassuring fantasies about what being a writer would entail slipped away. The reality loomed: read, write, edit, read, write, edit, sulk, discard, repeat. For some, this was a good thing, since they realised they didn't want to be writers anymore. For some, it was a bad thing, if they realised they did.

I hope that, for the readers of this anthology, you find fiction that makes you excited by the possibility of what these writers might do next. I hope that, for this year's graduates, you have all emerged from the course with your dreams appropriately modified. Remember though, that when you are within earshot of an undergraduate it's vital you maintain the façade that this course has given you access to a tunnel leading directly to Stockholm, and the offices of the Nobel Prize.

....

J D

Joe Dunthorne

Introduction

Henry Sutton and Jean McNeil

Where does fiction come from? Fiction is an imaginative enterprise, but it is also generated by observation and lived experience – by life.

This year our cohort of Masters in Creative Writing students include a circus performer, a mathematician, a computer programmer, a former stylist for the comedian Eddie Izzard, and a successful screenwriter. Is imagination the engine of life – outlandish and irrational as it is – we wondered – or is life the driver of a more coherent imaginary?

At UEA we never teach our students how they should write, or even worse, that there is one way to write which we privilege above others, but rather we enable the voice and inspiration our writers bring with them to the course from the bizarre pageant called life. We believe in and encourage innovation and flair, just as much as we nurture the quiet but telling line. Our principles have always been excellence, coherence of intent and deftness of control, plus intellectual depth and integrity.

As well as being a laboratory for experimentation, the course also has the capacity for prescience; present and future trends of fiction are being invented under our noses. This year in class we talked a great deal about the importance of and difference between style and voice. We seem to be in an age of voice, we considered – not only the writer's unique voice, but a valuing of the ability to channel and ventriloquise points of view that are extreme, unsettling, transgressive. We also discussed at some length, in the seminar and in the notorious Grad

Bar, an equation the alumnus and Man Booker Prize winner Anne Enright once came up with: style is a blend of technique and the self.

Then there is that weird alchemy of writing fiction – how, in narrating, you discover things you didn't know you knew. These known unknowns – the wayward paths of the imagination, random intervention of inspiration, unexcavated strata of memories we didn't realise we had – constitute an essential surprise and revelation, and are some of the often unacknowledged reasons why we write fiction.

There was growing recognition, amid a sizeable cohort, of the importance of building plot, with all its latent or loaded desire and conflict. But also that story might be less event and more the energy generated by the unpredictable velocity of character and emotional intent, at least in literary fiction.

In some ways it doesn't matter whether in their previous lives our writers bankrupted themselves teaching English in Laos, skulked as a 'commercial officer' in the British Embassy in Nairobi, or were in flight from a failed career as a croupier in Monaco (all fictional scenarios, in case you were wondering). Imagination and experience are in unstable fission, and while it might seem an everyday observation, we were astounded this year at the breadth and variety of what we call fiction, as embodied by the work of our students. We are proud to present this anthology by a diverse and wildly talented group of writers. Some anthologised here have already been well and widely published; others are at earlier stages in their publishing (and public) careers. All deserve serious consideration, and should be applauded for their wholly committed and searching approach to fictional expression and literary culture.

· ·

H S, J M
Senior Lecturers in Creative Writing and Co-convenors.
MA Creative Writing: Prose Fiction, UEA.

Henry Sutton and Jean McNeil

Sonal Aggarwal

A Family Affair
An extract

The attendant packed the barfi and tied the box with a string. With the packet under his arm and a drizzle falling, Vinayak set out for Raani's house.

As he knocked at the blue door he wondered if he should have brought the sweets. But he was here and so was the barfi and there was nothing to be done about it.

Raani opened the door and stepped aside. He felt she had been expecting him. It hung in the air somehow.

'Where's your goat?' he asked, finding the courtyard empty.

'When it rains, she just goes into my room and refuses to come out. Her name is Lata,' she added. They walked across the courtyard to sit outside the bedroom, where the roof jutted a little, so that they would be saved from the drops.

The two watched the rain fall and the dust-coloured sky hang low with clouds. There was a patch of orange rain under the street lamp.

'I bought these in the market.' He gave her the sweets.

She untied the box. Her hair was loose and the raindrops had left dark spots on her green kameez. 'Barfi.' She smiled. She offered it to Vinayak and took one too. But as she bit into the sweet, she thought how he would not touch the water from her kitchen.

The house and the town beyond were silent. The rain fell in big drops.

'Do you not feel lonely sometimes, living by yourself?' he asked.

'I have Lata.' She looked down and scratched her toenail. 'When my husband passed away ten years ago and then my mother-in-law, the silence suffocated me. But it's strange how it grows on you and then almost becomes a presence, someone you can talk to, pass your time with.'

Vinayak pictured her in the house, late in the evenings, turning on the lights, moving from the bedroom to the kitchen to the courtyard, folding the washing, chopping vegetables, and the silence following her around.

'I can't imagine living alone.'

'When my husband wasn't having fits or obsessing with water, washing his clothes in the middle of the night, or bathing in the morning with five buckets of water, he went to a woman in the neighbourhood. Our fights were violent. I can't say I miss that too much.' She gathered her hair and started to plait it.

Vinayak watched her. 'Some said he was possessed by a spirit,' he said. 'But I think there were just some bolts loose in his head.'

'I could never figure him out. Still, after he passed away I sat at home just crying. Then my mother-in-law passed away too and I started working in people's houses.'

'Did you never want to marry again? How old are you?'

'I must be thirty now. Sometimes I wish my husband had at least given me a child.' She lowered her eyes and started to scratch her toe again. 'But I have Lata. It's OK.'

Vinayak leaned in and kissed her.

The rain sprayed their cheeks and clothes. They moved to the room.

When he was leaving she gave him a polythene bag to cover his head, so that he would not get soaked, but they were glad for the rain, for now no one would see him leaving her house so late.

Now every third or fourth day after completing the household chores, Vinayak would visit Raani. Her body seemed new to him every time they made love, made up in two shades, the stomach darker than the breasts, the thighs fairer than the calves. Afterwards, he would look at her as she lay by his side, trying to imprint the colour palette of her body on his mind. It disturbed him though when she asked him to leave her a mark on her lips or neck or breasts, something that she could return to when he was away. He would laugh it off and tell her not to be childish. He thought about her constantly when they were apart, but never told her that. Raani would bathe in the afternoon after coming back from work and darken her eyes with kohl and put on glass bangles, and wait for Vinayak. It pleased him to see her make this effort. He was an old man, and didn't know what she saw in him, why she would even want him. In the evening, before he left, they would eat together in the kitchen. He taught her how to soak a slice of bread in sweet milk and fry it, like Sumitra. Raani looked forward to this half an hour as much as the lovemaking. Vinayak moved with ease through her house now, in and out of the kitchen, or lounged in the thin courtyard with Lata blinking sedately. One day he bought an exhaust fan for the kitchen, and put a twenty rupee note in her palm to send for the electrician later. When Raani folded her fingers over the note, it quietly changed something between them. She started to defer to him on small and big matters of the house. Vinayak had never known what it was to be a part of a house or someone's life in this way.

*

'Where were you the whole afternoon and evening today?' Sumitra asked Vinayak, as she sat in the deep cane chair in the kitchen, sipping tea. She was familiar with his habit of lingering in the bazaar, chatting with shopkeepers, sitting five minutes here and ten there. But these long spells of disappearance over the last few months were new.

Vinayak glanced up from the cauliflower that he was chopping. He wondered if someone had told her about Raani. 'I just stopped to watch television in one of the shops,' he said. 'And I didn't realise how late it was until I heard the temple bells.'

Sumitra took a sip from her cup. She watched him as he sat on the floor, one knee folded under the chin, back against the wall, separating florets from the cauliflower. She felt there was a new calmness about him, a sense of being settled.

*

Raani's sister came to visit her, and for two weeks Vinayak did not see Raani at her house. They met for an afternoon at the edge of the town where a stream flowed and farmers grew beans and peas in small patches. The two sat under a tree and ate the roasted chickpeas that Vinayak had brought along, and looked around and smiled at each other in between. It felt strange to be together outside. It felt like they were lovers.

'Do you think you'll marry me?' she asked.

He continued to chew on the chickpeas in his mouth, though his jaw moved sluggishly and self-consciously now. 'See, how heavy their school bags are,' he said, pointing to the children trudging down the road.

*

Vinayak lay on the charpoy in the courtyard. Raani sat on the floor cutting reeds to make a broom. When twenty brooms were done, she would sell them to a shop in the bazaar. She looked up from the reeds, and said, 'Stay the night.'

'That won't be possible.'

'Why?'

Her insistence irritated Vinayak, but still seemed to fill the distance that he had felt the whole afternoon, even when they were in bed. She had seemed coiled in a shell, while he lay bare next to her. He turned now on his side. 'You talk like a child.' He smiled. 'What'll I tell Sumitra and Madan where I am going?'

'They don't own you, do they? Or is it that you don't want me to have the slightest claim on you?'

'We're together now. How is spending the night any different?' He slept with her, ate with her. It didn't matter to him anymore that she was a low caste, that her forefathers had cleaned toilets with their hands. Sometimes he thought of marrying her. Renting a room in the town and settling down with her. Leave for work in the morning and come back in the evening. Or live with her in his room on the terrace. Sometimes it seemed so easy. But he knew Sumitra would not let her into the house. And what would Raani do after marriage? He wouldn't want her to continue cleaning people's toilets. He imagined her wilting on the terrace in the heat and growing bitter and dry and brittle from it. He thought about this often but could never come to a conclusion. At this stage of life, he only wanted peace of mind, and love too. He knew he was being selfish. And it troubled him.

He got up and put the charpoy against the wall. He looked at Raani, but she didn't raise her eyes from the reeds. He quietly closed the blue door behind him as he left. Overhead, a batch of sparrows flew home.

That night as he stood outside Madan and Sumitra's bedroom filling the air cooler with water, he heard Sumitra tell Madan that he had been away the whole afternoon again. 'Do you think he's searching for a new job?'

'Where do you think he'll go after all these years?' He heard Madan laugh. 'This is his home.'

These words said even without thinking warmed Vinayak's heart. He felt angry with Raani. Her face, as she sat making the broom, swam before his eyes. He drowned the image in the air cooler and fixed the shutter back.

A week passed and he did not go to see Raani.

It was Sunday and Madan was reading the paper in the bedroom, when Vinayak walked in with the duster. He started to dust the cupboards and then moved to the side tables. 'Sit down for a minute,' Madan said and put the paper to one side. Sumitra had told him last night that the vegetable seller had told her that Vinayak went to Raani's house every afternoon. Vinayak sat down on the edge of the bed. He feared what he thought could be coming.

'So what's this I hear about you and the sweepress?' Madan folded his arms across his stomach and waited for Vinayak to talk. His dark face bore chicken pox marks. Winter or summer, he dressed up in safari suits in shades of brown, pants and shirt cut from the same heavy fabric. As a young man, he campaigned for local politicians, and still spoke as though he was on stage. Being a sweet maker had never fitted his ambitions. He knew he would have to close down the factory soon. He wanted to start life all over again, see what America had in store for him. He wouldn't mind working in a shop or even driving a taxi, if it came to it.

'I'm sure you are not thinking of marrying a sweepress,' Madan said. 'You should put an end to all this. It's gone on for too long. I don't want to say too much. You are an old man, wise enough to know good from bad, I hope.'

Vinayak got up and started to dust the side tables. He felt angry with Madan and himself. He wanted to see Raani. He wondered if she would be upset with him for being away for a whole week.

'You can't marry her if you want to live in this house,' Madan said, as Vinayak left the room.

Sonal Aggarwal is working on a collection of short stories. She grew up in India and holds an undergraduate degree in Economics from Delhi University. Her writing has appeared in *The Caravan* (India), *Open Wide Magazine* (UK), and *Grey Sparrow Journal* (USA).

Alita Balbi

The Immortals

*This is a work of fiction. Any similarities
with reality are mere coincidence.*

It took twenty-five years and the need for a UK visa to persuade me to go to Rio de Janeiro. My boyfriend, Heitor, had never been there before either, so he was incredibly excited. The truth is that I was always afraid of Rio, of all the violence we heard about every day in the news. But this time I had to go, and so we went to stay for three days in my cousin's flat in the city centre. My cousin worked, and her boyfriend, Răzvan, offered to show us the worthwhile attractions. Since Heitor and I were both literature students at the time, Răzvan thought it was obvious the first visit should be to the Brazilian Academy of Letters.

When we got there, my first impression of the building was that it was unimpressive. But so are most libraries and anything related to literature in Brazil – the National Library is beautiful, but we're not actually allowed to walk through its corridors, so it doesn't really matter how wonderful it is. The BAL building is actually a house, a pale yellow house with square windows and columns at the front, mimicking classical Greek architecture. Except it was built by the French as an unfavourable copy of one of their palaces.

The entrance was at the side, because I guess the main one is only used for big events, most of which I imagine must have nothing to do with literature. The reception is dark and bare and, on the day we visited, it was being kept by a grumpy guy who talked to us in a way that made it clear he would rather be sleeping than seeing our eager faces.

'They're not from here,' Răzvan told him, 'I brought them to see the place.'

The grumpy guy appeared to be containing a laugh, and I wondered if he thought it was funny to have someone actually wanting to see the Academy – I don't know if that was the reason, but it's what makes sense now. We had to turn in our IDs, and he told us he would have to keep them while we 'looked at the place.' He then picked up the phone and called someone. This someone was another grumpy sleepy guy who, judging by his face, had clearly been taking a nap at the back. He took our bags and said we could get them back when we left. Even though I felt severely unwelcome there, I kept my hopes up that all those requirements were due to the highly valuable items we would find there.

The grumpy sleepy guy accompanied us to an elevator that took us one floor up. Leaving the elevator, we saw a small room with nineteenth-century-style chairs and a Persian rug to our right. Răzvan told us it was where the Immortals (that's what the members of the Academy are called) have their afternoon tea. I kept wondering if any of them actually troubled themselves to go. Then Răzvan took us to the left, where we entered a relatively small room with big wooden study desks at the centre and books on shelves that encircled the room. I asked Răzvan if that was it; if that was all there was, and he said yes. At that moment, we were approached by a grumpy angry guy who asked where we were from.

'Minas Gerais,' Răzvan said. 'I live here now, but these two are just visiting.'

'But they are so white,' – the guy looked at me and then at Heitor – 'I thought they were foreigners.'

I wanted to tell the guy that there are actually white people in Brazil, but I knew he wouldn't take it lightly.

'What do you study?' he asked.

'I'm doing my Master's in Brazilian history,' Răzvan said.

'We're doing ours in literature,' I said.

'What kind of literature, specifically?'

'He studies war literature and I study women's literature.'

'What war? What women?'

'Second World War. Sylvia Plath.'

The guy gave a sarcastic laugh. 'But these are not Brazilian things,' he said. 'You come from Minas Gerais. You have great women poets in Minas Gerais, and no one even knows about them.'

I wanted to tell him I knew them, but I didn't really like their work, and that was no one's fault really. Instead, I just said: 'It's not my thing.'

'Not your thing ... I see. That's why Brazil is the way it is now. See all these books?' He looked around, and I just wanted to ask if he thought that that was a lot. 'They are here gathering dust because no one comes to read them. I've worked here for more than thirty years and it has always been like this. People here don't care about their culture. They are only interested in what comes from outside.'

None of us answered. Even Răzvan, who was usually so articulate, just nodded his head and looked away. We had planned to stay there for a bit, but gave up on the idea. We got back into the elevator and arrived at the reception. The grumpy sleepy guy gave us back our backpacks and IDs. On the reception walls I now noticed the pictures of some of the Immortals.

'Who knows – maybe one day you'll be an Immortal?' Răzvan said.

I felt as sad as I ever had before.

Epilogue: A Panorama of Brazilian Literature

'No one can tape another person, take an interlocutory conversation and disclose it without the authorisation of Justice, especially something said by a senator of the Republic, who has a privileged forum by the Supreme Federal Court.' Immortal José Sarney: politician whose name was mentioned at various corruption scandals. Still alive.

'There is nothing completely wrong in the world, for even a broken clock is right twice a day.' Immortal Paulo Coelho: guru of popular sayings and known for using other people's lines. Still alive.

'We kill time, time buries us.' Immortal Machado de Assis: one of the few great Brazilian writers, died in 1908.

'What really matters in the end, to live or to know you're living?' Clarice Lispector: one of the few great Brazilian writers, died in 1977 without ever becoming an Immortal.

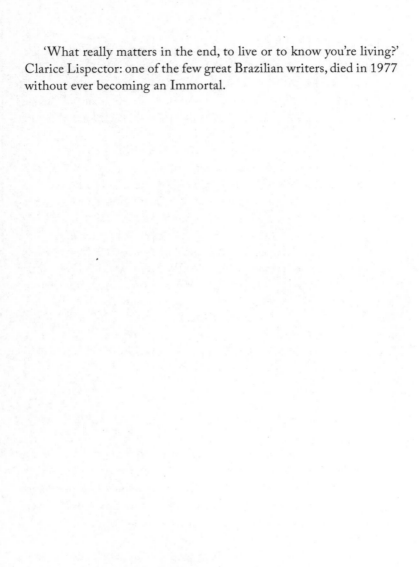

Alita Balbi grew up in a small town in Brazil. A life free of drama and excitement made her turn to writing at an early age. Her writing explores the difficulty of communication in today's relationships, especially in the context of a more and more technological and globalised world.

Oonagh Barronwell

Awe and Wonder

A dome rested on a pavement for seven calendar days amid the passers-by. Larger than a cloche but just as smooth, it was thought best to be metallic against interested foot-taps and the boys of the area who, predictably, jumped on and attempted to cleave it from the ground with straining fingers clawing into its base. The dome, however, was fixed firmly and would not budge.

On day eight a small square door opened in the side of the dome, noticed by the man who owed the Everything Shop outside which the curiosity had appeared, and a silver shaft emerged from it holding an opaque crystalline ball of aquamarine. Barney hadn't seen it happen, but upon consideration remembered that he had seen it happen, and recounted the insidious motion in excellent detail.

'It just came out!' he told Bernadette and her daughter, each highly affronted at the case.

After that there was no stopping. Next came a marble of mercury, two separate fists of red stone, a flat, crescent-shaped disc and two sand-encrusted gobstoppers of different sizes, each on its own protruding rod. By day seventeen a further appendage had surfaced with a bulbous orange ball-bearing attached, and since there were now too many pieces to relate to individually, the people of the road traded names for the entity in its wholeness, or Barney's Pimple, and several knelt on the pavement to push faces up close and examine the growing spot.

The nodules and openings, the little rounded doors, every aspect of the item had been meticulously polished and dragging fingers lightly across its surface revealed that careful tracks were impressed in the metal in regular circles, and that one final door lay waiting to open.

On day twenty-one Barney knew he'd heard a ticking, and had the dome not appeared in this particular community maybe would have called the police. But sure it's doing no harm; so they let it remain.

Day twenty-five saw Nicola from the *Telegraph* arrive with an A5 notepad, but it had rained on days twenty-two, -three and -four so there was really nothing to be said; rainwater had just spilled from the doors and the entire gadget seemed unaffected. Day twenty-six, however, produced an egg of pearlescent green and blue topped with a cap of snow white.

'Oh mommy Joe it looks like our child's mobile,' Danielle exclaimed on her way past with baby in the pram, and the next day made the same announcement to the queue in Delaney's Fruit Shop.

'Aye right enough.' Mr Delaney handed over the change for an orange. 'Matches this girl's coat too.'

The girl smiled. She took her money, holding the coin in her hand only to reveal it suddenly – flash! gone! – from her opened palm. Only baby in the pram noticed. The girl smiled again, found the missing coin perched amid a trio of plums and dropped it into the baby's cup.

'Mickey!' Danielle heard the splash as the girl left the shop, walking toward the dome.

'Here –'

Next door someone stopped a blue-haired lady, on her way into the chemist, and they each watched as the girl in the midnight blue suit knelt down, took from her pocket the lightly pockmarked orange and plonked it on a small spike now visible on the top of the dome.

Rising, the magician proclaimed:

'This, good people, is the machinery of awe. Come my friends and witness for yourself that which you already know, that we are living a life of amazement!'

She lifted the dome from the ground and at her touch the planetary arms began to tinkle and move, circling the orange sun as each turned on its pedestal.

'I am Andromeda, purveyor of natural magic, and this is known as an orrery. With it you can touch the stars and feel again your childhood wonder. You madam, please, come and see, come and reconnect!'

The blue-suited girl reached out to the woman poised at the chemist door, shining, holding the dome with arms outstretched.

'Missus, I think she's talking to you.'

'Mm-hm,' droned the woman, pressing at the edges of her lips as she adjusted the handbag in the crook of her arm. She had to advance.

The embroidered sequins of the girl's blouse mirrored the light glinting off the dome; she was the moon drawing a blue-haired meteoroid ever closer.

'Wonderful. Now, look into these skies. This, dear lady, is our solar system. Here we are on this little nickel chunk and it rests snugly in a bowl of space. Look upward with me – do you feel the light on your face?'

The magician held up the orrery, still tinkling and revolving, searching for the angle which would catch the light and illuminate the woman's neck as she peered upward, but her subject then stepped back slightly and drew down the sleeves of her polyester coat.

'Well, these very beams have just travelled over ninety three million miles to land upon you, and in just eight minutes. Imagine that! Recall what you were doing eight minutes ago – at the same time this light was leaving the surface of the sun! And feel how warm it is on your hands, on your face; how hot it must have been when it left!'

The magician paused, suspended in inference, but the meteoroid's orbit was set.

'Aye OK love, well thanks very much –'

The gaggle of onlookers shifted in their clothes. Some of them looked away. A man tapping a mobile phone lifted his head, glanced over, continued to walk beyond the crowd.

'I see you are not yet enthralled. But hear this: the stars of the night sky are a vision of history. As you look into the heavens you are time travelling, seeing the past, as things were millions of years ago. Not only before you and I were born, but before all human beings, animals and plants, the mountains and the sea,' her eyebrows arched to brighten her eyes even further, 'before the earth itself ever existed! Everything you stand upon and have ever known as your home –

right there, pre-dated by the night-time stars!'

A woman at the front of the circle made a little hoot of approval, at which Barney nodded sagely. 'That's right, sure I heard that the whole universe is moving away – the moon gets further away every year.'

'Yes sir, yes! Exactly right! How extraordinary, how ponderous to think!'

'Not really like.'

The magician looked at the two teenage girls snorting into their chins, then turned back to refocus on the blue-haired meteoroid, standing now with arms pressed by her bosom. The magician leaned towards her and spoke intimately, directly.

'You, dear lady, comprise cosmic dust. Every stitch of your body is a piece of the universe, boiled up and splurted out from a star. Building blocks that cooled, and because they did, now you are.'

The orrery whirred between them. She pressed on each word: 'The iris of your eye is a supernova explosion forever captured in time.' Her own enormously round eyes, unblinking; her best illustration.

The blue-haired woman's face fell backward into politeness. A laugh to signal retreat.

'See to be honest love, I've no idea what you're talking about.'

A measure of the expectation which had bound the group fell away. The pressure to understand was now anti-climactic, needless.

'I'm sure it all makes sense to somebody' – a murmur from behind her – 'aye, somebody clever like you, but I'm not one for all them big ideas. Can't be doing with it to be honest.'

Danielle and Barney agreed alongside: 'Aye, leave it to the scientists and philosophers, people trained in that kind of thing.'

'No, no, not at all! This is what I've come to show you, that all of these facts – the basic truths of our existence – are as relevant to you as they are to me, to our families, our dogs, to all of us anywhere around the world! You don't need to be a scientist – no one is unaffected by this knowledge, and in fact we have a say in it all!'

A boy cycled past on a children's tricycle. 'Aye your ma?'

The blue-haired lady glared at the boy, his knees peddling as high as his chest. The magician continued quickly, undeterred.

'Look. Consider the satin strands woven into this blouse. It cannot fail to amaze you that these fibres are made of the same materials which form the rings of Saturn? Picture it – a giant, satin-wrapped ball! Or that the steam that rises from the kettle you boil for your cup of tea is just like the gas swirling around Venus, right now over a hundred million miles away?'

She was trying, truly trying now, but the connection refused to form.

The magician reached for a final link, spotting the chain around the woman's neck with a miraculous medal resting above the woman's heart.

'I see you are a woman of religion. A woman of faith. You're used to believing without seeing. Well all that I have said does require a leap of faith, but only to see, to see clearly, the facts as they are. To think on them and ponder, to consider how special you are just because you are and how unlikely was your creation, to look around and absorb it all and realise that you are! You're a part of all of this! How wonderful, how beautiful! Such reason for great awe!'

Entrusting the orrery to the hands that would catch it, she thrust it into the air and flung her body to the sky – insistent, emphatic, triumphant, Ta Da!

The patter of hesitant appreciation. A few hands prompted automatically to clap.

The girl brought her arms back down to her sides. The woman with the blue rinse smiled consolingly.

'Don't worry about it love. You always knew I'd be a hard one to crack. But you did your best though.'

'Yeah.'

'Right, will we go home? You left a bit of chicken out for your tea didn't you?'

'Yeah.'

'Ach now, don't get annoyed about it. You knew it's not easy.'

'I know, I just thought this time, like with everybody there, I just really wanted to connect –'

'I know, I know.' She nudged her daughter's arm, making the effort to walk a little closer. 'Sure we'll get a chip on the way back round, that'd be handy.'

'Yeah OK.'

A cat watched them from its seat on a pillar between two railings.

'Ach look there's Schrödinger – come on mister, what are you doing away out round here?'

Watching the trio recede, Danielle handed the orrery back to Barney.

'Ach bless them,' she said.

'Ach I know. Sure we all try our best for each other, don't we?'

'Aye.'

'Amm, aye,' said the baby in the pram.

· ·

Oonagh Barronwell was born in Belfast in 1986 and when she is not selling literary crafts in a pop-up shop, ad-libbing as a Creative Writing tutor or opening a restaurant, she is working on an allegorical novel involving awe, quantum physics, a child prodigy and sleight-of-hand magic.

S H Binney

The Storyteller's Failed Apprentice
An excerpt

'Hiya! Back! Got a pal over, lassie fae school, be up in ma room!' Fatima shouted, all in one breath, as we went inside. She pushed me roughly towards the stairs. On the way up, I only caught a glimpse of the inside of her house: deep yellow walls, and, through a half-open doorway, bookshelves, full to bursting.

'Ma granny's here,' she said quietly, pushing open a door. 'She's dead traditional – wouldnae like me havin a boy round. Thinks it's a fuckin' disgrace if she sees me even like walk near one.'

I nodded uncertainly.

All the houses on our street were built to the same plan. Fatima's bedroom, on the left of the staircase, corresponded to mine, so I almost expected to see my blue curtains and posters when we went in. The walls were off-white, like mine, but there was a mural on one of them: two trees growing up from the floor on either side of her bed. They had smooth bark, and several thin trunks, branching out from the bottom and twining upwards into two huge fan shapes, full of green leaves and round red fruit, which didn't quite meet in the middle above Fatima's pillow. There were birds in the trees and, as I looked up, more bright birds flew around the room, painted on the walls and ceiling.

'Oh, ma dad painted that when we moved here, it wis fir ma weest sister,' said Fatima. 'But now Ah'm here. Ah wis gonnae paint over it but Mum wouldnae let me.'

'What would you huv painted?' I asked. 'They trees are great!'

'Aye, they're awright. You get used tae it. They're a bit ... Ah dunno.

I wanted jist the birds on like a blue background – it's no like they fly around on a bloody cream sky is it! An nae trees, jist sky. Especially no fuckin' pomegranates, nasty tastin' fuckers!'

'Ah've never seen a pommy-granite tree.'

'Me neither.' She sat down on the floor, cross-legged. 'So,' she said, looking at me, 'are ye gaunae tell me all about it?'

'Awright, fine,' I said smiling. I sat down beside her, our backs to the pomegranate tree furthest from the door, and began.

'Once upon a time ...'

'Aw fir fucksake, jist tell it normal, like,' she said, pushing my shoulder.

'Am are!' I pushed her back, but too gently. 'That's how ye dae it, in storytellin'!'

'Naw, jist tell me how it started.' She folded her arms, frowning at me.

'Aye, that's whit I'm daen! Ma ain way, right?' I wanted to push her again.

'Fine. Better be good then.'

I began again.

'So, it started in the summer, when the Storyteller first came over, I'm just like sitting in the front room and he rings the bell, I didnae even recognise him at first, stood there aw scary like, an he comes in and asks ma folks, can I apprentice yer boy, and they were like, whit Tommy? but he's rubbish, basically, and then they talked, fir ages like, that's what it felt like anyway, hours an hours, and then eventually they all come out and that wis me! Except, wait, ma folks hadnae seen him before, so off they went, had a right good time like, thought he was dead good, so then we started lessons, it was proper weird at first, right, 'cause ...'

My words were like a train, slowly firing up, awkwardly shifting gears and registers, then moving off clunkily, joltingly, before speeding up and smoothing down. I described the hillside where we'd had our first lessons, the wind and the cold and the shouting; I recited the Burns, and the Shakespeare, and told her how the sounds felt in my mouth; I told her about the winter evenings getting earlier and earlier until we were working in star-lit darkness out on the hilltop. At first I watched Fatima, looking for reactions, a smile, a flicker of her eyes;

but after a while I lost track of her responses and began to enjoy myself, talking to the whole room, and just to myself. I described the absolute darkness of the room in the Storyteller's house; I tried to fit words around the movements I'd enacted there, the ape-like and stooping things I'd become; I tried to make them fit a pattern, a progression, and make more sense than they did. Fatima listened and laughed, and made me recreate it: 'show me the ape-thing', 'show me the old man'. I smiled, and acted it out, high on her praise. Then I told her about the woman with heels I'd failed to become. I hadn't meant to. I just didn't want to stop the story. Her eyes were so big and interested and, for once, unaware of their effect. So out it came. Her laughter sounded like a siren.

'I'll show ye how tae be a fuckin' lassie,' she said, leaping up and rummaging about for her highest heels. I watched her, apprehensive, trying to grin back. Trying not to watch her for more than what she was teaching me as she walked, swinging her hips and pointing to her feet. Then she turned to me. I shook my head and protested, but when she started putting the strange shoes on my feet herself I gave in. I put the shoes on, smiling along with her, trying to ignore my unease. They cut into the backs of my heels, and did funny things at the toe, and felt like they didn't fit even though we were the same size. I stood up and wobbled, making us both laugh, but as I felt my hips move and my back change position I stopped and looked at her, unsmiling. What was she doing to me?

Her dark eyes glanced back at me, ignoring my expression. She appraised my womanly walk, nodding and prodding me to make adjustments.

'That's better, eh. Make a fuckin' awesome lassie now!'

'Aye, but, I wis telling you the story ...' I felt on display.

'Aye, awright, cairry on then.'

I kicked off the shoes and sat down again. I settled on the floor and crossed my legs. I was uncomfortably aware of my body, still lankily boyish. I wasn't sure what to say.

She asked about the Storyteller, what was he like, what did he look like. I absorbed myself in recreating him, showing her, from the safety of the floor, his mannerisms, his voice; I described his car, his house, his ridiculous phone; I told her about his impatience, and his rare praise. And as I spoke I changed him, adding lines he'd never said, removing actions that didn't fit, making him an easier character, with simpler characteristics and weirder gestures, to make me seem a better storyteller. I found it so easy, to invent him, and I relished it. My telling grew sleek and assured; I began to enjoy it again.

Before I'd finished we heard a slow thumping sound coming from beyond the door. Fatima grabbed me, looking round at the door, listening.

'It's ma granny,' she hissed. 'Stay there, hide behind the bed.' She jumped up, and was scrabbling around in a box by her bed. 'Here. Now act, right? You've got tae be a lassie now.' She shoved something on my head. I felt it; it was a hairband. I brushed my hair across my eyes. Her gran was calling. I moved over to where Fatima had been sitting. My coat and shoes, unavoidably masculine, were safely behind the door. Fatima looked over, and nodded. 'Jist yer face,' she whispered.

'Fatima!'

'Aye, Gran,' she said, opening the door and smiling sweetly. 'Can Ah get ye anythin'?

'No, I just wanted to see how you and your friend were getting on.' She stuck her head round the door, a wrinkled face surrounded by a black headscarf. She smiled, but her eyes darted around the room. I thought she was trying to catch us out.

'Awright, Granny. This is ah, Tamsin, ma pal fae school.'

'Nice to meet you, Tamsin, was it? And whereabouts do you live?' she asked. They both looked at me.

'Jist down the road,' I said. My voice felt strange. I tried to smile.

'Oh, how lovely. You must see Fatima all the time, then.' She beamed at me. I nodded back, smiling with relief.

'Ah wis jist gonnae make a cup of tea, you want some?' Fatima said, moving into the doorway.

'Thank you,' said her gran. Fatima propelled her out of the door, giving me a fleeting thumbs-up.

'Here, let me help you down the stairs,' she said; and they were gone.

I sat, waiting for Fatima to come back with the tea. The hairband was digging into my head behind my ears. I tugged it off, and threw it on the bed. I felt a little sick.

Footsteps were coming back up the stairs. Fatima appeared with two mugs, laughing.

'That wis great!' she crowed. 'She hadnae got a clue!' She sat down, a little closer to me than before. As she handed me the mug, our hands touched. We clinked our mugs together like adults drinking wine, and laughed. I tried to take a sip, but it was far too hot.

Fatima put her mug down. I remember how serious her eyes were, how I tried to find somewhere to put my tea, how it spilled and burned my hand, how it didn't matter because of the softness of her skin on my face as she kissed me.

S H Binney was brought up in Scotland to an American mother and an English father gradually going native. She studied English and French at Oxford University, where *Fig.* magazine published one of her short stories, and has worked as a teacher, a carer and a library assistant.

Daisy Bourne

Astley

An extract from a novel on the birth of circus

What I know is this.

The people of Lambeth call my father the Centaur.

In three days we sail to Versailles. The moon is not full but its light is reflected on the flat, dark water of the Thames, which flows inexorably to meet the Channel; the charts are criss-crossed with lines signifying the currents, to whose tug and pull we must attend like the soft mouth of an unbroken horse.

My first memory: he lifts me onto the back of his charger, Gibraltar, gifted to him by General Eliot on his return from Prussia. It is not white; rather, a mixture of mottled greys and black flecks, which, I will learn, are camouflaged with whitewash before every show. I grasp the withers, handfuls of wiry mane cutting into my fingers.

I feel its breath in my legs.

The walls stretch upwards, the rows of empty benches repeating to infinity, and then the sky beyond, gathering up a storm over Halfpenny Hatch. Drops of rain explode onto the sawdust, and my hands come away white. My father murmurs at Gibraltar's head and the horse, which a moment before had seemed as immovable as the earth, now dips and ripples beneath me like water. I look between the ears, curved like twin scimitars, and the horse lets out a bellow which gathers in my ribcage until I can hardly tell which one of us is roaring.

You've heard the stories: the horse, rearing with fright, falling from the troopship at a Hamburg port, that my father dove in after and swam back with, against the tide, his hand grasping its bridle; the charge at enemy hussars during which his horse was shot from under him; latterly the showman of London, riding two horses abreast along the highway, one foot planted on each of them, his voice bringing it all to a standstill.

Or perhaps it's the story of the diamond ring you're familiar with, chanced upon at Westminster Bridge, its glittering inlay catching his eye from the mud, that began it all?

Listen: there was no ring, at least not of the type a rich man wears on his finger.

The first act I performed, aged eight, was a re-enactment of the Titan wars against the Olympians. As I repaired the costumes and washed the paint off the horses, I envisaged the titanic scribe seeing the funeral parade return. He goes to his tablet, chipping the first mark to tell of their defeat, and then he pauses, recasts his chisel and while acrid smell from the pyre stings his nostrils, writes of the victorious homecoming of the Titan.

Within the year, Gibraltar was dead. My father ordered a roof built over the structure, blocking out the changeable clouds, and a man named Charles Hughes came to work for him.

Let me tell you how it goes.

Entrée

It begins on Midsummer's Eve in 1759, a hundred and fifty miles northwest of here in a town built on the banks of the Lyme, on a night when two paths are laid out before us and everything is possible.

Young Astley does not hurry home, though he should have been back at the workshop hours ago. Instead, his hands bear the tang of saddle soap and horse spit from the coach house, and the smell makes him resolute.

He climbs in through the narrow window at the side of the workshop, landing with a scuff of sawdust. The silhouettes of lathes and augers hang above the bench and he waits for his eyes to adjust to pick out any visions of his father hiding in a darkened corner behind a half-constructed cabinet, chisel in hand, eager for its flat edge to connect with the soft skin at the back of his knees. But there is nothing, and he opens the door into the cottage. Lizzy, his sister, sits at the scrubbed table, head bent. She could be his mother, except that he remembers leading her through the long grass by the banks of the Lyme on the back of a Saint Bernard. She had been small then, sliding around on the dog's narrow back, cheeks pink and grass-lashed.

She looks up at him with their father's pale eyes.

He talks quickly. 'I'm going South, Liz. With a fine gentlemen, or at least one in possession of a fine pair of warmbloods.' The feverish urge to laugh runs through him.

'So – what? You've come to bid me a tearful goodbye?' She shakes her head. She is standing now, hands tented against the tabletop. 'Come in, quietly, before you wake him.'

'You have woken him.' Edward is leaning heavily against the doorframe, grey hair tufted up on one side. On somebody else it might look comical; on Edward it lends him a demonic air, like a Beelzebub's horn. He lurches into the room, into the light, and Astley sidesteps him.

'That's right, always dodging: your responsibilities, your family, honest work. You've made it into an art, sure enough. You'll be going nowhere.' He takes the strap from the mantelpiece and winds it around his fist. It has been years since Edward was able to get him across his knee, but Astley still feels a mixture of fear and shame at the sight of the leather strap, the way a dog recognises the boot that finds the tender place between kidney and rib; his father favours stealth attacks of late, and is creative with his choice of missile.

Edward's nightgown barely covers his crotch, the hem trembling somewhere above his pale knees. The sight makes something collapse inside Astley, and Edward, who has been sidling towards him, chooses this moment to dart towards Liz. The strap strikes her on the cheekbone and sends her reeling.

'Couldn't dodge that, could you son?' Edward taps his temple with a crooked forefinger. When Astley starts towards him the old man flinches back but his laughter doesn't stop. 'Go on,' he says, spittle flicking from his teeth. From across the room, Liz watches them. The swelling is rising already beneath the welt, a thumb's breadth shy of her eye.

The gentleman's name is Lancaster, and the horses are warmbloods from German stock that he's hoping to sell into the regiments as cavalry. They are joined by two dozen fellow pilgrims, and along the way other contingencies travelling south are absorbed into their herd. It is safer this way, and invites camaraderie, among men and equines alike. Their company brings the children running out of the houses when they ride through the villages, hooves clattering on the cobbles and bouncing off the houses like the sound of applause. Arriving in the inn at Tamworth, there are boys not much younger than Astley, waiting to lead the animals, fetch water and rub salve into the cracks of the saddles and rub the horses down with wisps.

They reach Coventry at the end of the week, arriving at the horse fair as afternoon blends into evening. The smoke from hundreds of campfires drifts over the town. The horses prick their ears, flicking them back and forth in the haze like great moths, and rumble deep in their throats in reply to the sounds of their kin. It is another sound which speaks to Astley, his mouth and eyes and hair full of dust, blisters on every limb: above the calls of horses and of men, the dissonant strains of a string instrument and straggling voices, comes the clang of blades. They are singing to him.

The company gather on the banks of the River Sowe. Astley has never seen so many horses together in one place – pied ones with wall-eyes, barrel-bellied ponies and enormous shires, feather trailing in the water like seaweed. There is the smell of hot earth, mud, sweat and wet horse as they jostle to the bank. Astley's yearling approaches with its neck stuck straight out in front, making puffing noises which make Astley bounce in the saddle.

He plants himself in the mud at its shoulder and they move forwards together until it is fetlock deep. Its nostrils flare, and it lets out a bellow which makes Astley's ears hurt, then dips its head to drink.

There are shouts from the water, and the horse whips its head up so fast it narrowly avoids hitting Astley in the face; Grisham is on his feet in the middle of the river, where a rise of stones and gravel mean the water, in places, is shallower. In one hand he holds the reins, which are taut because the foam-flecked head of his horse is straining in the opposite direction, ears flat against its skull. In Grisham's other hand is his whip. At the other end of that is a cowering bundle of rags, atop a horse so emaciated that even with the proximity of the commotion, it stands, head lowered, the tendons in its neck standing out. It has expended all its energy taking a sly kick at the shiny chestnut gelding, and has now withdrawn, once again, from the world, leaving its owner, and engineer of its misfortune, to deal with the consequences. Water flies in a glistening arc as Grisham strikes the rag man with his whip, then turns his attention to the bony horse, striking it on the face. It screams like caught rabbit.

In the morning, Lancaster, Grisham and Astley go the Boar's Head where the recruits, tempted by cheap beer and displays of swordsmanship, are queuing up to enlist.

'They may look appealing now,' Lancaster says to them. 'When you're waist-deep in mud and surrounded by the enemy you may think differently.'

'Or I may not,' says Astley.

'That's true,' says Lancaster. 'Most likely, though, you won't get time to think anything at all.'

'Planning to become a redcoat, are you?' says Grisham to Astley.

'I might be.'

Lancaster shakes his head and continues to pull knots out of the manes with a stick.

'He won't,' says Grisham.

When their turn comes, Astley mounts the yearlings, and one after the other, takes them in circles. Their ears flick back, listening for him, and away again to the men in red coats whose eyes look out for swollen tendons and signs of balking.

'They're from exceptional stock,' says Lancaster. 'Sire's a German charger.'

Colonel Eliot considers; they have no shortage of offers, though most of the animals are good only for cannon-fodder. The queue stretches to the road – though he is still below quota – his beer is unpleasantly warm and he is coming out in a sweat rash beneath his uniform. But Lancaster is right; the horses move well.

'Angelo,' says Eliot, and a small Italian-looking man approaches the yearlings, running his hand along their shoulders to let them know he is there, before leaning down to feel their legs. Astley watches. The horses dwarf the man, but he blows gently into their nostrils and they lower their heads; he sticks his thumb in the gap between their wolf teeth and molars, tickling their tongues with a forefinger so that they open their mouths, exposing curved brownish teeth. He checks for filing-marks, and, satisfied, nods to the Colonel.

While they barter, Astley steps up to the aide-de-camp and offers up his name.

'Age?'

'Seventeen, sir.'

'Your profession?'

'An equestrian.'

Grisham snorts.

And the officers exchange looks, wondering at the audacity of this tall, lanky youth.

....

Daisy Bourne lives in Norwich with her partner, who is a mind reader, and their three-year-old son, who isn't. From a family of artists, she performs in circus and cabaret shows throughout the UK and abroad, and is also working on a novel about the anatomy of a family, told through objects.

Nic Bouskill

Exit Wound

Simon's running fast, tearing through crowds of screaming kids. He's all elbows and knees and panting like a dog. His shirt is short, shorts are tight, because it's the end of term and Mum says they'll have to do. His hair clings to his sweaty neck in damp rat-tails. He's chasing Nadia.

Break should be footie with his mates, kicking shins, but he can't take his eyes off Nadia's flashing heels and floating hair. She's quick and light and skips and swerves and his longer legs don't compensate. Kiss Chase is a stupid game, but he hasn't got the words, hasn't got the moves, and today's the last day, his last chance. But dark-haired Nadia won't be caught.

She keeps twisting away but he's got to get her, he's got to, even though he has no idea what will happen when he does. He'll grab her by the hair if he gets a chance, yank her back and put an arm round her throat.

She stumbles and he's almost on her, but she snakes away, spins through a group of blank-faced boys, leaps over crouched kids, and Simon barges after, marbles skittering away as the players holler. He's not Simon anymore, he's possessed.

But at last she slows, she's stopping, she turns towards him. He crashes into her and they almost go over as he wraps his arms around her, bangs his chin on her forehead, searches for her face which she thrusts into his armpit and her hair is everywhere, in his mouth. She shrugs and wriggles but he clings on. She pulls her head up, looks at him with her bright, dark eyes and he doesn't know what to do.

There's a red mark on her head where they met. Other girls would cry but he's never seen Nadia cry. She shrugs herself free and stands there and they breathe at each other.

Nadia's really Gary's girl. Simon sat on a bench yesterday and Nadia slid over to talk to him, then Gary came up and thwacked him on the side of the head, knocked him over backwards, his ear throbbing, and it sounded like he was underwater. Gary grabbed Nadia and sauntered away, and Simon took himself off to Mr Evans. Today Gary's suspended.

So Simon stands there with his throat full of spit. Break's nearly over. He doesn't know what to do and he's got no breath left to say anything. Nadia bunches her dark, wavy hair behind her head, then she looks around, grabs his hand, jerks him forward and he follows at once, past the low wall at the end of the playground. They slide down the bank, knees buckling, then they're away across the field, cut grass sticking to their soles and then flying off in lumps. They keep to the edge, Nadia reaching out to brush her fingers over the hedge that has oily leaves you can scratch your name on. They're out of bounds. If a teacher sees them ... but today, the last day, nobody cares.

They reach the stand of trees at the far side of the field. It's where the smokers go at lunchtime. They run into the shadows and he's panting again, but they're under cover.

Nadia crouches down and crawls under one of the bushes. Simon sits, avoiding the brown cherries in the matted grass that leave marks on your bum. Nadia comes out of the bush backwards with two fag butts. She slips a hand underneath her skirt and pulls out a lighter. Simon's been told that smokers die, but dying today means no comprehensive in September, no bogwashing and no bullies. Nadia holds both stubs between her lips. The lighter won't spark first time, but soon there's a flame. He watches his hand go out but it's awkward taking the glowing inch without burning himself. He sucks on it hard, like Coke through a straw, then coughs and retches and Nadia smiles. Simon feels the smoke rise inside him.

The bell rings. It sounds all right from down here, like a posh doorbell, not like when you're up close. So that's it, he thinks. Through the leaves Simon can see the other kids forming lines. Soon they'll walk up the steps and through the double doors towards problems and handwriting and the playground will be empty.

It's going quiet. Simon listens to a lawnmower on the other side of the hedge. Nadia stands up, takes a couple of steps away from Simon into a bright patch among the leafy shadows. She looks at him for a moment. There's a plate of glass between them. She turns to face a tree, takes a skipping step and drops her hands to the ground, arches her back as her heels find the bark. She holds the handstand, elbows locked. Her skirt tumbles down from her waist. There's a patch of wavering sunlight on her thighs.

She drops down, comes up in the right order, covered again, Nadia again.

'You like it?' she says, and Simon nods.

'I can take my knickers off,' she says. Simon shakes his head.

'Gary likes I take my knickers off,' she says.

Simon realises he's not Gary. He'll never be Gary. He yearns for problems and handwriting.

'We're going to get into trouble,' he says.

'No problem,' she says.

'Let's go back,' he says.

Nadia sits down away from Simon, starts tearing up grass, throwing it over her shoulders. A distant plane rumbles. It's a beautiful day.

'Do you really have no parents?' he says. Simon's dad moved out three months ago. He sees him on Sundays. He's not told anyone.

She keeps on tearing. 'Yes, no,' she says.

'What happened?' says Simon.

'War,' she says. 'Shit war.'

'Who looks after you?'

'My uncle and aunt. They OK. But old, not funny.'

He wants to ask her if she really takes her knickers off for Gary. It seems impossible.

She smiles at him. 'You good boy,' she says. 'You worry little things. I don't. Not no more.'

She starts making a daisy chain. She has long fingernails for splitting the stalks. Simon picks daisies, drops them by her knee, but she ignores them, keeps on picking her own. Simon wonders what their class will be doing now. Maybe helping Mr Evans take down the displays. Maybe solving riddles like the one with the fox, goose, and grain. He remembers the present for Mr Evans in his desk.

He turns towards school and sees Mrs Cook coming down the steps. 'It's Mrs Cook,' he says.

'Shit,' says Nadia. 'She's bitch. Come on.'

They plunge into the bushes, full of the sharp stink of cat and fox. Spiderwebs snag Simon's skin as they push branches out of the way. It's gloomy inside and at the back there's a chain-link fence. He thinks they'll hide, but she ducks down and clambers through a hole.

'This way,' she urges.

He puts his head down, shoves his shoulders through, crawls forward and draws his knees behind him.

They are in a garden. His shoes sink into soft soil. It's overgrown with nettles and brambles dotted with tight red blackberries. Clouds have buried the sun and the air is cool on his legs and arms.

'Where are we?' says Simon.

'Home,' says Nadia. She finds a stick in the weeds and swings it in swift arcs to fell the nettles that threaten the narrow path.

Beyond the garden, the house is dark and derelict, the windows smashed and the upstairs frames charred, the walls filthy with soot. Tattered red and black curtains hang out of the downstairs windows.

'We lived here, before the fighting. Don't you remember?' Nadia scythes her way forward. 'We had goats, greedy smelly creatures. And a few chickens. Look, here's the run.'

There's a tangle of rotten wood and plants and chicken wire.

They walk towards the house, Nadia slashing nettles. Simon stands on a piece of yellow newspaper that crumbles under his feet into irregular brittle flakes. There are words he can't read. He looks up and catches a flicker of movement in the corner of his eye. The house. Is someone up there? He thinks of Gary.

'Nadia,' he whispers urgently. 'Up there.' He points. Nadia comes over to him, puts her head close to his, and follows his line of vision.

'Is it Gary?' says Simon.

Nadia shakes her head. There's a ghostly shape in the dark room, the glint of something poking out. Then a flash and a CRACK next to Simon's ear like a firework. He flinches, blinks.

'Shpejt!' says Nadia. Simon doesn't follow. 'Quick!' She pulls him through the nettles, they brush his arms and legs. An angry buzzing thing zips by with a SNAP. They run through the half-open door of a shed. There's no floor, just earth. There are sandbags piled up against one wall and they drop behind them. Dirty light filters in through the cobwebbed window.

'What is it?' says Simon.

Nadia's trembling. 'Snaiper,' she whispers. He opens his mouth but she puts a finger against his lips, shakes her head. 'Little brother,' she breathes, 'Mosubenimerak.'

She takes both his hands in hers, grips them tightly. 'I won't let them take you this time,' she says. Her eyes are wide. The words trigger a vision, the back of a lorry, the stench of an oiled gun, dogs on chains. He thinks it was a film he saw. He looks out at the garden, hoping for Mrs Cook. The nettle stings throb like lashes. He holds his breath, squeezes Nadia's hands.

The window explodes and the air is full of fragments. Nadia's face sparkles, with tears or shards of glass he cannot tell.

....

Nic Bouskill was born in 1969. He spent the eighties studying, the nineties travelling and the noughties teaching. He is currently being educated by his four-year-old son, Tristan, and supported by his wife, Ping. He is writing a novel, *Bonding*, about hoarding, sibling rivalry and James Bond.

Elizabeth Briggs

North-North-West

An extract from a novel in progress, set in Oxford in 1935

C hristiana has been for a walk. When she arrives back at the house she takes off her gloves and leaves them on the hall table. She will go and sit in the drawing room. Since Mrs Cunningham has told her what a nice place it is, she has taken to spending time there. If she sits there enough, perhaps she will begin to believe it, to deceive herself. The drawing room door is open. She hesitates on the threshold, walks in. Heinrich is standing there. He is never there; he is always in his study, always. He only ever comes in if she is already there. She does not know what to do or where to sit.

Look, he gestures, his voice brighter than usual. Stollen, in Oxford. A miracle.

Oh, she cries, seeing the tea tray with the cake sitting on it, nestled happily alongside the cups and saucers and the teapot. She runs and kneels on the floor beside the table, leans in to the slice Heinrich has already cut to smell the lemon zest and spices and icing sugar, presses the soft sponge, scoops out a fingerful of marzipan. Different to the Stollen back home, but still recognisable.

Where did you find it, she says, sucking at the raisins and candied peel stuck between her back teeth.

There's a bakery off St Giles's.

She picks up the knife to cut herself another slice. Mama always cut it at home, and she used to sit impatiently at the table waiting to see how big the slices would turn out, as the knife in Mama's hand hovered and hesitated and sank into the cake.

She puts the knife down at the thought of Mama. Heinrich stands beside her, munching and murmuring with satisfaction.

Everything all right love, he asks, looking at her.

Yes, I've just had enough.

Well there's plenty more if you change your mind.

Christiana goes to bed early that night without having dinner, leaving Heinrich in his study working away into the night. She lies alone in the bed trying to prise a currant out from between her teeth with her tongue. She doesn't want it there anymore. She sticks her fingernail into her gum, scratching at it. During the Christmas season when she was little Mama had sometimes given her a piece of Stollen with a cup of hot milk in the evenings, as a treat. She used to lie in bed afterwards running her tongue over her teeth in search of the last traces. But now she doesn't want to taste it. She has brought the memory of Mama and home into contact with Oxford, and now the memory is tainted and spoilt. She realises now that memory and the past do not travel, that they must be kept locked up preciously, unspoilt and untainted by any association with this place. She has learnt her lesson now, and will not make that mistake again. Heinrich meant well in buying the cake, he meant to cheer her up and make her time in Oxford better by bringing her favourite memories into it, but she wishes he hadn't done it.

She flings back the sheets and runs across the cold corridor into the bathroom, where the nausea rises in her throat and she vomits up the cake into the basin.

The next day, Christiana meets Mrs Cunningham at ten minutes to four at the Walton Street tea shop, and they walk to Roger's studio. The house in which he lodges is tall and thin, with a top floor perched up high, twin windows facing out over the street. Mrs Cunningham rings the doorbell with Roger's name on it, and after a couple of minutes Christiana hears the inner door scraping open, and a rattle of the lock being undone. Roger's head curls round into the open space, and he smiles.

Come in, he says, holding the door open.

He leads them through a hallway and up two flights of stairs. Christiana hears the noise of a family somewhere else in the house, and is disorientated for a moment, unsure of whose house she is in and who lives where.

I live just up here, Roger tells them, gesturing to one final flight of stairs.

Christiana looks upwards. She can see the sky out of a high round window on the landing above, and she quickens her pace as she follows him. All three of her homes in Berlin had been upper-storey flats, and neither she nor her friends ever manoeuvred their lives across different levels of a single house as she is forced to do in Oxford. Roger's flat becomes Berlin now, a home which exists all on the same level. As she climbs higher and higher the view from the round window expands, and she can just see over the curved sill and down over a moving street of people, their foreignness suddenly forgotten in the familiarity of her vantage point. The flat smells of paint and some kind of chemical spirits, quite different to any other smells she has encountered since coming to England.

Roger leaves them sitting on a sofa in the studio, and Christiana looks around her at the paintings hanging on the walls and propped up on the floor, tries to see what they all are without craning her head too obviously. Mrs Cunningham appears happy to sit still.

The family here are very nice, says Roger, carrying in a tray of tea things from the kitchen. Very accommodating. He pours out the tea splashily.

Christiana looks across the room to the twin sloping windows in the roof.

Have you seen the view? Roger asks her. Come and see.

She is happy that he has noticed her interest, and she comes over to where he is lifting the latch and swinging open the window.

Here, stand on this, he says, pulling forward a low chair.

Christiana sees that the chair is upholstered, and she glances at her shoes and hesitates.

It's fine, he tells her. I stand on it all the time.

She puts a foot onto the chair, a hand on the sill, and swings herself up. The cold air blows in her face, and she leans forwards to see down over the street. It is a miniature town, and she feels as if she could reach down and pick up any one of the people taking tiny steps along the street, toy baskets and parcels in their hands and doll-sized hats on their heads. A ribbon of bicycles weaves along the road, and her eye skims after them.

Do be careful Christiana, says Mrs Cunningham's voice from somewhere behind her.

She looks at Roger, but he shakes his head and so she stays up there, though she puts both hands on the window rail as an acknowledgement of Mrs Cunningham's warning.

Roger climbs on a chair and pokes his head out of the adjacent window.

Look, he calls out at her emerging head, pointing. There's the university press. And over there, see, is the book shop. And down there is —

A gust of wind blows and she can't catch what he said, but she nods at him as if she has, not wanting to break up the flow of conversation by asking him to repeat himself.

Two birds soar across their view, from one treetop to a further one, and Christiana almost laughs at the sight. A larger bird flies after them, and the sky is suddenly threaded with winging birds.

Roger climbs down from the window and helps her off the chair. He closes the windows and turns back to the table where Mrs Cunningham is still sitting down, and hands Christiana her cup of tea.

That'll warm you up, he says.

When she gets home she sees a round tin on the table in the kitchen. She opens it, and finds inside the rest of the Stollen. Heinrich must have put it in there. She looks at it and begins to cry, silently. She cuts a sliver off the end and puts it in her mouth and chews it.

Late one morning the next week Christiana hears noises coming from Heinrich's study. The door is open, and she wanders by to see what is happening. Heinrich is putting some papers in his briefcase. A photograph lies in the centre of the desk. He looks up at her and smiles. She moves towards the desk.

What's this? She reaches for the photograph.

He picks it up and holds it under the light, studying it closely. Herman sent it over, he says.

She sees a letter open on the table. She has not heard from any of her friends back home.

It's an interesting thing actually, he continues, turning the picture this way and that under the lamp, eyes fixed on it. They found it in a Sicilian excavation, but it's almost certainly Nordic in origin. We've no idea why it was there, how it got there. There's nothing that points to a Nordic presence on that site.

This was the only thing?

Yes, completely out of place. I can't explain it.

He takes a seat to hold the photo closer to the desk lamp, still turning it around and around, examining it from every angle. You know, he says, this could be a really huge moment. Finding out how it got there may point to some great pattern of migration and movement of peoples, something we've never heard of before, something really significant. I honestly think it might be a spectacular discovery.

He stands up, knocking the chair to one side as he moves. Christiana puts out a hand to catch it and reposition it.

Anyway, Robert and I are having lunch in college. I should go. He picks up his briefcase. Goodbye love. He kisses her on the cheek.

She keeps her eyes down, and he leaves the room. When she has heard him go down the stairs and out of the front door, she moves nearer to the table, puts out a finger to touch the photograph of the alien hairpin. It lies oddly in a hollow of the rock, like a fissure.

Christiana is sitting in the drawing room that evening reading Mrs Cunningham's book of Keats when she hears a nasal grunting sound from outside. Without seeing, she can't decide if it is barking dogs or geese returning home after the winter. She loves the sound of geese flying away in autumn and returning in spring. If it is geese that she can hear, they will soon be gone, and she will need to get outside quickly. She goes and rattles at the front door latch but it doesn't give way.

Heinrich, she calls, hearing him walking down the passageway behind her. How do I open it? Let me out.

Heinrich makes a murmur and she hears him move towards the door. He takes his time, and she rattles at it again.

How do I open it? she repeats. His hand appears and twists the lock and pulls it open, before disappearing again as he walks away down the hallway.

As soon as the door opens she hears more distinctly, and it is not the growing and fading lilt of geese, but the grounded hoarse rivalry of dogs. She steps out alone onto the stone path and listens to them calling out in the night. She can't see them; the noise comes from beyond the trees. She wants to stay with them, to feel less lonely. If she waits long enough out here something is bound to happen. The street can't be empty for this long, endlessly empty.

She begins to shiver, and the dogs give up barking and go silent. No one has found her. She walks slowly indoors, turns back towards the gap in the hedge where the pavement is visible beneath the street lamp, but no one comes, and she can't see anything, and she steps in and closes the door. Back inside, Heinrich is nowhere to be seen.

....

Elizabeth grew up in Oxford. She studied English at Cambridge, following this with a Master's at York. Last year she took a poetry course run by Oxford University, and her resulting portfolio won the university's Mawby Prize for 2011-2012. She is currently working on her first novel, provisionally entitled *North-North-West*.

Sean Colletti

···

How to Begin a Short Story / Garage Sale

T he alarm clock was literally next to his ear.

*

The Writer knows that it cannot begin with waking up, even though people often wake up. The Writer considers the use of the word 'literally' echoing the beginning of another story. The Writer decides that if waking up was an acceptable beginning, a small enough percentage of The Readers would know that story to warrant keeping the reference. The Writer makes note of this in The Writer's Notebook.

*

He was literally baking by the pool.

*

The Writer acknowledges the similarly effective use of the word 'literally' without beginning The Story in a less-than-desirable context. The Writer wonders about forcing in the word 'literally' to signpost literary influence. The Writer suspects usage of a pool and a warm climate to be suggestive of material that is too autobiographical or that could be interpreted as autobiographical, and The Writer does not want The Reader to think The Writer is accustomed to 'baking by the pool' when The Writer is, in fact, accustomed only to 'baking.' And not literally.

*

The snow creaked shut under his footsteps.

*

The Writer knows this is good usage of metaphor, because the sounds of snow underfoot and closing doors are comparable enough, and the image of closing doors with each step – especially if the main character is walking in a residential area – is strikingly visual. The Writer wonders if the sound of snow underfoot is different to a masculine ear than to a feminine ear. The Writer does not want to infuse gender politics into The Story, so The Writer chooses to avoid forcibly adopting the feminine perspective, because The Writer feels more at home in the masculine perspective, and, besides, The Writer has already chosen to avoid some autobiographical material and can justify the use of it in this case.

*

The snow creaked shut under his footsteps. It was only five more minutes until the bridge.

*

The Writer will avoid usage of a bridge, because The Reader has already made comment on The Writer's tendency to write about suicide, and there is no telling what The Story's main character will do at the bridge other than commit suicide, because The Writer knows that characters have a tendency to do things independently of The Writer, except not really. Bullshit, actually, The Writer thinks, but best to avoid bridges altogether.

*

The snow creaked shut under his footsteps. It was only five more minutes until he got there.

*

The Writer is fully aware that 'there' is vague, especially in relation to 'five' very specific minutes. The Writer also now hates the snow metaphor. The Writer thinks it is maybe the worst metaphor that The Writer has ever written, and that The Reader will also be very conscious of this. The Writer feels very impersonal about this beginning. The Writer wants all of this to be less impersonal.

*

I am stood watching my grandmother cook breakfast.

*

The Writer welcomes the immediate connection that The Reader will likely experience in the first-person, present tense narration of The

Story's main character, but The Writer laments the specificity of the eliminated 'five' minutes in relation to 'breakfast.'

*

I am stood watching my grandmother make quesadillas.

*

The Writer now welcomes the specificity of 'quesadillas' even if further specificity – such as 'chicken quesadillas' or 'bacon and tomato quesadillas' – could be achieved at no extra expense. The Writer worries about 'quesadillas' indicating geographical position in The Story by process of elimination, because The Writer is unsure as to whether or not geographical position – like gender – is of import.

*

I am stood watching my grandmother scramble eggs.

*

The Writer is pleased with the verb 'scramble,' which is more active and interesting than 'cook,' and The Writer nods The Writer's head in favor of the neutrality of 'eggs' that any component of The Reader should be able to relate to.

*

I am stood watching my grandmother scramble eggs. My grandfather is drinking from a can of beer.

*

The Writer again examines the issue of specificity in relation to 'a can of beer,' but concludes that adequate specificity is inherent in 'a can,' and, anyway, the detail may suggest to The Reader that The Story's main character is unable to distinguish between cans of beer or is otherwise uninterested, which would allow The Reader the benefit of assumption that The Story's narrator is of a young age – relatively – which would further distance The Story's narrator from The Writer and, in turn, veer The Reader away from giving that connection unnecessary and inaccurate import.

*

I am stood watching my grandmother scramble eggs. My grandfather is drinking from a can of beer. The telephone begins to ring.

It is only now that The Writer admits to having always hated 'I am stood' as a beginning – hate.

I am watching my grandmother scramble eggs. My grandfather is drinking from a can of beer. The telephone begins to ring.

*

The Writer wonders how many things The Reader will tolerate happening at once. What, is The Reader expected to believe that the life of The Story is so busy that three things must be happening immediately and simultaneously?

*

I am watching my grandmother scramble eggs. My grandfather is drinking from a can of beer in a way that suggests he has long since forgotten to be aware of when he is drinking alcohol – it has become an extension of him.

*

The Writer fears things have become too personal, because the detail of the alcoholic grandfather that has become a part of The Story will give The Reader more suggestion that The Story contains more autobiographical material than it actually does, and, besides, the sophomoric sentence is too long-winded for The Story, which is meant to be anything but long-winded, especially if The Story's main character is to be young.

*

Grandma is scrambling eggs. Grandpa is drinking from a can of beer.

*

The Writer celebrates replacing 'my grandmother' and 'my grandfather' for 'Grandma' and 'Grandpa,' due to the delay of establishing third- or first-person narration in addition to giving The Reader a suggested familiarity with The Story's characters. This is surely the best beginning that The Writer has ever written.

*

Abuela scrambles eggs while Abuelo drinks beer from a can. It is 6:42 on a Saturday morning, when Arturo-César should be asleep. But Mama dropped him off last night to help with the garage sale, which Abuela said she would pay him a quarter every hour for. Arturo-César does not know this is less than five percent of minimum wage. He does not know anything about percentages.

Abuelo watches TV, but he doesn't listen to it. He says that hearing aids are uncomfortable. But Papa says that Abuelo really just hates being forced to live with Abuela and doesn't want to hear anything she has to say.

'Tony.'

Abuelo continues not to listen to the TV or to Abuela or to anything but a low humming in his ears.

'Tony!'

'Que?' Abuelo burps. It smells like beer.

'Ayuda a Arturo.'

'Que?'

'Puta madre. The garage sale!'

'Oh.' Abuelo looks at Arturo-César and burps again.

There are blankets lying on the driveway. On the blankets are items for the garage sale. Arturo-César's older sister has offered some of her Barbies. Most of them he has de-limbed. There are clothes. Among them is Arturo-César's favorite shirt with holes in both armpits that Mama was saying she was going to throw away. Arturo-César waits for Abuelo to get some things from the shed before putting on the holey shirt over the shirt he's already wearing. The holes rip bigger.

Abuelo comes back with a weed-whacker and puts it on one of the blankets. The door to the kitchen opens. Abuela gives Arturo-César a scrambled egg and bean burrito.

'Gracias.'

Abuela does not look at Arturo-César. She looks at Abuelo.

'Did you put up the signs?'

Abuelo takes a swig from his can of beer. 'Que?'

'Letreros!'

'Oh.' Abuelo burps.

'Well?'

'No.'

Abuelo doesn't usually let Arturo-César sit in the front of his truck anymore, because Arturo-César once cried until Abuelo took him to get pizza and Abuelo told Arturo-César to stay in the truck and Arturo-César put the truck into neutral and the truck rolled into a wall. Abuelo said the repairs would cost a million pizzas. Arturo-César thinks he could eat a million pizzas if he was hungry.

Abuelo pulls over on Las Posas Road. He tells Arturo-César to go put up the sign with the address for the garage sale, but there are already lots of signs for other garage sales, Arturo-César tells him. Well then take those down, Abuelo says. But what about those other garage sales, Arturo-César asks, and Abuelo tells Arturo-César that all the other garage sales around here are at houses owned by gringos and that they don't need the money.

Arturo-César rips some signs off the pole on the sidewalk.

Someone has made an offer on the weed-whacker. Veinticinco dólares. Abuelo says OK and the man says he'll be back after work and Abuelo says OK again and the man asks Abuelo if he can put it aside and Abuelo puts it aside. After the man leaves, Abuelo puts the weed-whacker back on the blanket.

'What about that man?' Arturo-César asks Abuelo.

'Un pendejo. If he comes back, I'll call la migra on his sorry ass.'

'What's la migra?'

'The boogeyman.'

Arturo-César laughs at the face Abuelo makes. Abuelo was a bad papa and, looking at Arturo-César, decides for a moment that he doesn't want to be a bad abuelo.

'Ven aqui, mijo. You know why I would call the boogeyman on that pendejo?'

'No, Abuelo.'

'Porque es un enemigo. He forgets where he's from. And he lets the gringos piss on him. Your abuela and me, we come here and we took no mierda from no gringos. You should never take mierda from any gringos or anyone else.'

'Abuela says I'm un gringo medio.'

'Don't listen to your abuela. Someone should have told me that forty years ago.'

'Si, Abuelo.'

'You're a good kid, Arturo.'

'Si, Abuelo.'

Arturo-César and Abuelo are beginning to bake in the sun. The man has not come back for the weed-whacker. Abuelo sits on a lawn chair next to fourteen empty beer cans. Another man in a flannel shirt and baseball cap parks across the street and has a look at the assortment of things on the blankets. The man notices Arturo-César ripping limbs off Barbie dolls.

'What are ya'll selling here?'

Abuelo lifts the bill of his own baseball cap. 'What's it look like, gringo? Stuff.'

'Got any hunting kind of stuff?'

'Hunting? What you mean hunting?'

'Hunting. You know? Bang, bang. Deer and shit.'

'Deer and shit.' Abuelo stands up and falls over. Abuelo stands up again and goes through his toolshed and comes back with a machete. 'This'll get your deer.'

'God damn, Paco. I ain't looking to get into any hand-to-hand combat.'

'Not hand-to-hand. Deer and shit.'

'Ya'll got anything else?'

'What's this look like, a fucking thrift store? Arturo, we got any hunting shit? Deer and shit?'

'I can hunt deer on the Nintendo.'

'There you go, gringo. How much for el niño?'

'Pardon me?'

'El niño. Cuantos?'

Abuelo walks into the kitchen and knocks over a bowl of Abuela's fruit salad and then walks to the bathroom and pisses a third in the toilet, a third on the toilet and a third on the tiles. He washes his hands and goes to sit at the kitchen table to count his money.

Abuelo wakes up to the jabbing of Abuela's index finger.

'Que?'

'Donde esta Arturo?'

'Que?'

'Arturo!'

'Que?'

'El niño! Donde esta?'
'El niño …'

Abuela calls the police, hands the phone to Abuelo, runs out of the house and looks down the street where the truck has rolled.

Sean Colletti was born in 1988 and raised in Camarillo, California. He began studying mathematics there before moving to England to do a BA in English with Creative Writing at the University of Birmingham, followed by the University of East Anglia's Prose Fiction MA.

Paul Cooper

....

Untitled

*The second chapter of a historical novel set in
Polonnaruwa, Sri Lanka, in the year 1215.*

I woke up to the sound of shrieking. My first thought as I blinked myself awake was that I had slept through the morning, that I was late for a meeting with the king, and that my newest poem wouldn't be completed on time. It took a moment for that old, wonderful life to fall from me like water. There was the smell of smoke, and you were quivering beside me, already awake. I jumped as a scream, broken halfway by sobbing, came from a room some way down the terraces – there were the barks of foreign voices, more cries, and then a cruel eruption of laughter. It was then that I realised. I had fallen asleep, and the enemy had stormed the palace. Magha was here.

Through the floor, I could hear a man chanting the dharma in terror, getting louder and louder, then breaking off with the sound of clay breaking against a hard surface. From the street outside the window, there was shouting, the clatter of chariot wheels and hooves. Then dozens of feet pounded the steps to our terrace with the sound of leather on stone, and I tried to enclose you in my arms and cover your ears as the running and screaming grew closer. Then the door curtain screeched on its rail. A swordsman and two spearmen entered the room. They were bearded, with patterned sashes, and they had the yellowed eyes of men who have caught the sweating sickness more than once.

'Get up! Get up!' the swordsman ordered in Sinhala, then Tamil, with a mouth born into speaking neither. The men strode across the room to our mat, tearing down the curtains as they came, feet thumping on the boards and straw.

You sprang up as though you would fight them with your fists, but when I tried to stand, two of the warriors leapt at me and threw me back against the floor. My elbows cracked painfully against the wood and I saw the remaining soldier hold you by the wrists and laugh as you tried to strike him. My legs were kicking like a crushed mosquito until a cold, sharp line pressed at my throat. Everything seemed to stop. I'd never before had a sword held against my neck, and at any moment, I expected to feel a searing note of pain open my insides to the air, blood warming my chest.

'What are your names?' one of the men demanded, and the pressure lessened on my neck so that I could speak. A hundred lies flooded my head, but none of them reached my lips.

'I'm Asanka, poet to the court of King Parakrama Pandya,' I replied, my voice cracking. 'She's Sarasi, a servant girl. Please – ' but at the mention of my name, one of the men growled. Before I could beg them for our lives, the sword's edge pressed back against my windpipe. I could smell the smoke of campfires and half-cured leather, the rancid sweat on the man's body, the smell of horses. He said something to the others in a mainland tongue, perhaps Kalinga, and they laughed, looking first at me, and then at you.

'Don't touch her!' I tried to shout, but gargled like a man drowning. The man nodded down at me with sharp eyes, and said something else in his gorse flower language as screams and barks harrowed the air from outside. My heartbeat filled my head, and the soldiers dragged me along the floor and out into the sun. I remember catching a last glimpse of your eyes as you cried out after me and the remaining soldier threw you to the floor. Someone was squealing like a pig going to slaughter, and I realised that it was me.

Outside, the men pressed me against a pillar and tied my hands behind my back. I was pleading, mewling; tears were blurring my vision. I wondered where they would take me to die.

'I have money,' I kept saying. 'I'll give you money. Please don't kill me – you don't know what you're doing. I eat dinner with the lords every day, I've touched the king!'

Then the rope tightened, cutting a line of fire into my wrists, and they pulled me back towards the citadel and its servants' gate, laughing at my struggles.

'We're not going to kill you, little man,' they crooned in dislocated Tamil. 'We're taking you to the king. Have you ever been brought before a maharaja? Magha of Kalinga has summoned you, and now you have to appear!'

I howled and trembled. I felt myself faint, swimming in black water, and the warriors took my weight between them. Then we were in the palace: the world passed by as a blur of granite, red brick and plaster, angular entanglements of limbs, the sound of breaking wood and pots. We were moving at speed, and I remember detesting the bunches of flowering jessamine that hung everywhere, bright and immodest amid the horror. As the soldiers carried me up the palace stairs, the tops of my feet tapped against their sharp edges, step by step by step.

Soon, with my eyes scrunched shut, I heard the sound of a large door opening. I passed into shade, into an atmosphere of heat and incense, and when they dropped me I opened my eyes and saw that I was in the throne room for the second time that day. Cushions were scattered everywhere, an ornamental dais overturned and one of the curtains slashed with a sword, gaping like a laughing mouth. Tall foreign soldiers stood silently along the walls, with a line of bound and sitting lords, some weeping, some trembling on the floor.

King Parakrama Pandya was kneeling in the centre of the chamber, a swordsman on either side, his hands tied behind him. I forced myself to stifle a scream at what I saw. Blood was pouring down his cheeks, caking his neck and matting the plaits of his beard, still seeping from the meaty sockets where they had gouged out his eyes. He was murmuring softly to himself. He turned at the sounds of our entry, mouth gaping, and I'm sure that he looked right at me. I will see that face until I die.

Standing over him was a man in armour made of leaf-shaped plates, and a spired helmet in the Persian style. He turned his head as I entered, flushed as if from some intense task, and when he smiled it wasn't the kind of smile that some men flash like knives, moving only their lips, but a smile that cracked his whole face. This man, I knew immediately, was Kalinga Magha.

I still have a coin from those times, a treasure I keep wrapped in many cloths in the bottom of a chest. You can appreciate the skill of the mould casters in capturing the sharp lines of that face, the mouth framed by that moustache, and almost full with teeth. Of course, what you can't see in silver is his most commanding feature: that pair of thick, black eyebrows, black as charcoal, some of the largest I have ever seen. The soldiers who brought me bowed to their master, and one of them spoke. The Kalinga Prince nodded, and looked at me.

'You,' he began in accented Tamil, and it surprised me that his voice was as smooth as coconut water, each syllable placed like a game piece. 'You are Asanka the poet. Am I correct?'

I nodded, all words gone, and my soldiers pushed me towards him so that I stumbled. I was sure that I would be killed, and shrunk from the Kalinga when he turned to face me. Then he said, of all the things he might have said,

'I'm a great admirer of your work.'

I stung at what I took to be his mockery, but he was no longer smiling. He drew his sword and let it catch the light, placed it across his index finger and let it teeter there for a moment.

'You have perfect balance,' he said.

He snatched up the sword and handed it to one of the soldiers beside the king, who I noticed was mopping an inky fluid from his hands. The man put a whetstone into the cloth he was using, took the sword and began to sharpen it. There was no expression on his face, nothing. I couldn't take my eyes from the steel, and on the floor, King Parakrama shook with every scraping note it played. Magha walked across the room to the throne, and the king's table.

'I imagine that these are yours,' he said, and raised the pages that I'd left there that morning. Leaf veins, light through paper. He took my shamefaced silence as a yes.

'My name is Magha,' he said, 'the youngest prince of the Kalinga line, and, from today, ruler over the province that you call the Raja Rata. You should have seen this king, this man, come out to welcome me. He came out to give me his crown. How can he live with the shame? There's much to be done here, and a great king has to act quickly, to surround himself with talented men. Tell me: have you ever heard of the poet Sri Magha?'

I tried to say that of course I had, but as the sharpening of the scimitar continued like the scraping of a catgut string, and my gaze fell to King Parakrama, I could say nothing. The thought of you swam unbidden into my head – that you might already be dead or dying somewhere while I stood there and choked on a question that wouldn't make even my dullest apprentices sweat. I felt my knees almost buckle, and knew that if I collapsed with hands tied I would fall painfully. The Kalinga went on.

'Magha was the poet who immortalised the court of King Varmalata in Gujarat. He is the author of the holy Sanskrit epic, the *Shishupala Vadha* – surely you have heard of it. Magha. He shares my name.'

The way he said this made it seem a credit to the artist.

'Yes,' I managed. 'I've studied it.'

'Aha! He can speak!' the Kalinga said, his smile returning. 'Always a useful skill for a poet. The problem is, I can't read Sanskrit. It's a language of priests and philosophers, and I'm a man of action – but I've heard so much about this Magha, and this *Shishupala Vadha* in particular. They say it's the poem in which Krishna reveals all of his secrets. Your name,' the conqueror said. 'It's Sanskrit, isn't it?'

'Yes.'

'Do you speak it?'

'Of course.'

'As well as Tamil?'

'Yes.'

'And you are sure that you have read Magha's poetry?'

'Yes.'

'Excellent. Then you,' he said with much ceremony, 'you will be my royal translator. You will translate the *Shishupala Vadha* into Tamil in my name, and I will give it to the people of this land, this bud I am here to bloom. Thus we may achieve the king's pleasure and the greater good of the masses in a single move.'

'It's a noble cause, my lord,' I remember saying, and King Parakrama turned his face towards the sound of my voice. I imagine that if he still had his eyes, he would have wept.

'No no no,' Magha said. 'There are no noble causes, only noble men. What a day for lessons! Come, start with the poem's title. Translate it for me.'

I looked up and saw a spark in his eye. He already knew what it meant.

'*Shishupala Vadha*,' I croaked. '*The Slaying of Shishupal.*'

Magha smiled, showing his perfect teeth.

'The death of a king,' he said. 'That *is* a fitting way to start, don't you think?'

There was an almost imperceptible movement of his hand, and a flash of the sword. My old king fell forward, and blood glugged from his throat the way water glugs from a toppled jar.

. . . .

Paul Cooper grew up in Cardiff, Wales, and studied at the University of Warwick, where his interest in ancient mythology began. He wrote a novel during his time living in Sri Lanka. He loves to travel, and to learn new languages and alphabets.

Daniel Davies

The Past Shines

Although he would later turn to prose, Troy's first love was poetry. He once told me that he only started writing prose to fill the boredom between poems. Some he sent off to magazines, others he didn't. Some were published, most weren't. But what never changed was his passion for writing them. His only frustration was how few came to him. He had a favourite anecdote – Allen Ginsberg telling W H Auden that he aimed to write a poem a day. 'One a day?' exclaimed Auden, mock-horrified. 'Isn't one a month enough?'

Troy could only write poems when he felt 'inspired'. He used the word unironically. 'You have to be inspired. You need what John Ashbury calls "privileged moments". The poem has to come from somewhere. It needs a reason to exist.' Although he never used the word 'muse', he might as well have done, because what usually inspired his poems were women: whoever he was pursuing, or seeing, or remembering, at the time. In fact, it was usually the third scenario that got him writing. 'I sometimes wonder if I only go out with people so I can wring a poem from the inevitable break-up.'

One woman who inspired him was Kacey. How many poems he wrote about her, I don't know, but he told me he had over thirty. I know that some were published in small magazines, but not which poems, nor how many. He collected his favourites in a short pamphlet that he sent out to a handful of close friends, including me (what else should a sister be if not a close friend?). 'It ain't exactly *Birthday Letters*,' he wrote on the postcard that came with the pamphlet. 'But I've written worse, believe it or not.'

Yet the aftermath of Troy's split from Kacey wasn't just poetry – it was also good old-fashioned heartbreak. I'll never forget the email he sent me. I was sitting at my desk at work, about to go into a meeting, but I just had time to skim it. How did it go?

Hang on. Rather than recreate it from memory, I'll see if I can find it in my Hotmail account. I'll sign in and do a search. Give me a minute.

Found it:

Chlo, Sorry to email you out of the blue like this, but i just feel so low. i emailed Kacey last week and have had nothing back. I emailed her again last night (I know , i know, but I miss her so much) and still haven't heard and now I feel so hurt . it seems she wont even respond to my emails now. I feel fucking awful, it makes me want to leave Prague. Plus theres no one here this weekend. a few other teachers are going to Cesky Krumlov for a couple of nights but I've been so many times already and i don't feel like going anyway. It just means I'm going to feel so shitty . i don't know what to do. Sorry to bother you like this, just didn't know who else to turn to
   T

As soon as I finished reading, I knew what I had to do – fly out to Prague to see him. Troy never gave explicit cries for help, but this was as close as he'd get. (His slapdash typography, if nothing else, showed that he wasn't himself.) I went to my meeting feeling tetchy and worried. When I got back to my desk, I booked a flight online: from Gatwick to Prague on Friday night.

*

Seventy-two hours later, I landed at Ruzyně airport. The instant the glass doors opened, I saw him. He was leaning against a chocolate dispenser at the back of the arrivals hall, reading. I stopped for a moment and thought of my last visit to Prague – and of Oxford train station more than ten years earlier. Memory on memory: a palimpsest of Troys. Whenever he met me anywhere, he was always early and always reading. He couldn't get enough of it. Nor could I. We lived for literature. What was between us, in Tony Harrison's words, were books books books. But they didn't divide us, as they do in Harrison's poem; instead they joined us, bound and stitched our lives.

The first thing I noticed was that he'd put on weight. A lot of it. He must have been two stone heavier since I'd visited in May. Although he was wearing a parka, I could see that his face and neck had thickened. Looking down to read his book, he'd gained an extra chin. For the first time in his adult life, he looked his age. Gone was his boyish litheness, which had perennially made him look five years younger. He was as chubby as I'd ever seen him. My challenge, as I neared him, was to pretend I hadn't noticed.

When he looked up and saw me, his arms fell to his sides. Then he wrapped them around me as if I were a life raft. His book slipped from his hand and landed at my feet. I ignored it and closed my eyes. He smelt of chlorine, cold air and, faintly, fried food.

'Good to see you,' I said.

We hugged for a full minute. Even through his coat, I could feel the new flesh on him, the barrel-like curve of his stomach. But when I loosened my grip, he tightened his. He pressed his face deeper into my neck; I felt a wetness on my skin. I hate it when men cry – it knots my stomach – perhaps because they find it harder than women, which always makes it feel more serious. The only time I ever saw my father cry was at Uncle David's funeral.

'I'm so sorry about Kacey,' I said. 'I wish there was something I could do.'

I could feel his palm in the centre of my back. 'You've done it.'

We disentangled. I picked up his book from the polished floor and handed it to him. 'Don't forget this.'

'Oh. Thank you.'

I looked at its cover: *Too Loud a Solitude* by Bohumil Hrabal. 'Czech?'

He nodded. Whenever Troy lived abroad, he'd immerse himself in the literature of that country.

'Any good?'

'Very,' he said, wiping his eyes. He frowned at the book, holding it in both hands, his face growing intense; I could always distract him with literature. 'And very weird. About this bloke who works in a paper-crushing plant under a repressive regime, which is clearly Communism. He's supposed to pulp all the books that come his way, but he saves as many as he can – a kind of bibliophile Oskar Schindler. In fact, maybe that's the whole allegory?'

He looked up at me and smiled. Even with the weight he'd gained, Troy still looked beautiful when he smiled – all white teeth and sharp green eyes. He was one of those people whose smile begins in their eyes, whose eyes are its epicentre; then the smile spreads downwards, like a blush of happiness, as though the mouth were following the eyes' example.

'I'll have to read it,' I said, linking my arm through his. 'Come on. Let's get out of here.'

Stepping outside, we were buffeted by a Siberian wind. It was only just November, but winter had settled in. Taxi drivers in sheepskins stepped towards us, quoting prices with icy breath puffs. Because Troy didn't earn much, I offered to pay for one. But he refused the men in Czech: 'Ne, děkuje.'

'Fuck it,' I whispered, 'let's get one.'

He shook his head. 'Nah, waste of money. I told you that last time. The buses and trains here are brilliant. It's not like London. Say what you like about totalitarianism, it produced some cracking public transport.'

We caught the 119 bus from the airport. The passing suburbs were hushed and dark. Sparse snowflakes swirled in the air like blossoms. At Dejvická, we scuttled down into the metro station. We took the green line to Muzeum, the station nearest to Troy's new flat. Twenty minutes later, we emerged into deafening traffic. It was already ten o'clock.

'Wanna go for a drink?!' Troy shouted.

'Nah, I'm knackered! Let's just go back to yours!'

We didn't have far to walk. Troy's flat, already the fifth he'd lived in during his two years in Prague, was on a central street called Žitná. He shared it, he'd told me, with a gay Canadian called Brie ('Like the cheese,' he said). But she was spending the weekend in Riga with her Latvian girlfriend.

I was glad to escape the noise and cold. The flat was roomy, sparely furnished, with wooden floors and glass-panelled doors. The glass rattled as we walked. Our voices echoed slightly. The windows were double-glazed, keeping the rooms toasty, but letting in the rumble of traffic. I shed my bobble hat and duffle coat. Troy took off his furry-hooded parka. Underneath, he was wearing a black Pink Floyd T-shirt.

It was then that I noticed his arms. A sciatic shimmer went down the backs of my legs. Below his left elbow were what looked like slash marks. Some were scabbed and dark, others fresher and reddish. They weren't particularly striking; in fact, in the flat's murky light, I might even have failed to notice them. But maybe, subconsciously, I'd been looking. Because I remembered seeing similar marks on my last visit to Prague. Back then, Troy had explained them away as scratch marks from metal football studs and I'd chosen to believe him. Would I believe him again? Dread filled my stomach, like bad milk.

He hung up his parka and turned to me, hands on hips. I met his eyes brightly – I didn't want him to see me looking at his arms. Yet if he hadn't wanted me to look, why had he worn short sleeves?

'So what can I get you?' he asked. 'Beer? Tea? Coffee?'

'Tea would be nice.'

'Čaj. Coming up.' He gestured to his bedroom, whose door was open. 'Go through. Have a nose around.'

I did. A typical Troy room, it had an air of being temporary. He could have packed up and left in ten minutes, like a fugitive. There were few pictures, apart from a couple of photos on the windowsill. Piled on the floor, like three miniature towerblocks, were books in Czech, German and English. There was a rucksack and an open suitcase in a corner, which still had some clothes in it. Beneath the long window was a radiator, as pale and bulky as the backbone of a dinosaur; a pair of swimming shorts was drying on it. Beside the window was a wooden desk with a folded chock of paper under one leg, like a wobbly table in a café. On the desk were a laptop and printer, surrounded by pages. The pages were covered in Troy's handwriting: insertions, deletions, diagrams. Was that his screenplay?

I went to the window, perched on the armchair and parted the metal blinds. At the top of Žitná, the traffic lights were changing. I watched cars power down the street in one direction, like stampeding cattle. Shamefully out of date, and influenced by Cold War documentaries I'd seen at school, I still imagined the Czechs driving tinny little Ladas. But they'd long since upgraded to Mercs, Beamers, Audis. It sounded like a grand prix down there.

'Shit,' said Troy. 'No milk.'

I turned round: he was standing behind me in the doorway.

'Don't worry, I'll have it black.'

'No you won't. I'll pop out and get some.'

'Troy –'

He silenced me with a held-up palm. 'Seriously. There's a Vietnamese joint on the corner. We'll need some for breakfast anyway. I'll be five minutes.'

I shrugged. 'OK.'

He whirled his parka on, as if it were a cape, and left the flat. I opened the blinds fully by twisting a metal rod. This time, instead of looking down, I looked up. The sky above the city had cleared: a curved, starlit absence. My eyes fell to the city itself; my mind wandered its onion domes and rooftops.

Daniel Davies was born in Birmingham to a Welsh father and Polish-German mother. He studied English at Cambridge. His many jobs include sub-editor, copywriter and English teacher. His first novel, *The Isle of Dogs*, was published in 2009. At UEA, he's been working on another, *The Past Shines*.

Michael Durrant

Sand

He has left instructions for his mortal remains to be cremated and for his ashes (if it is possible at this point to speak of 'his' mortal remains, 'his' ashes) to be cast, for sentimental reasons, across the dunes at a particular spot on the Norfolk coast. He has left these instructions knowing that they cannot be fulfilled. He has left these instructions knowing full well that they cannot be fulfilled exactly as he has prescribed. But at least the intention is there. He understands, from his point of view, the point of the gesture. This is what is important. Yet he also knows that from the moment (or perhaps even long before: the whole plot sabotaged from the very beginning) the urn is collected by that individual, or group of individuals, entrusted with the task of delivering his ashes to the prescribed location, they will (his ashes) be already conspiring to drift somewhere other than their intended resting place. This he has anticipated. His uncle, Terence, worked for a time as a furnace operator at a crematorium and explained to him once (his uncle was drunk and had embarked on a lengthy reminiscence which, though agonising, at least saved him, the nephew, the effort of having to speak) how sweeping the ashes from the oven was an inexact science, with a good proportion lost down cracks, inseparably mixed with other ashes, caught by draughts and blown into the air, or otherwise inhaled, the thick masks given to the operators to avoid this regrettable inhalation of the dead often having to be removed because they inhibited – what with the furnace making, to use his uncle's words, 'one hell of a racket' – effective communication between operators. Even were the ashes to survive intact, find their way 'whole,' as he wishfully imagines it, from the furnace into the relative safety of a plain, unadorned urn, those entrusted (that word again) with transporting them to their final resting place, as per his painstakingly detailed instructions, might very well decide that the weather is too poor that day, rendering the whole operation unfeasible; they might get halfway to the coast and pause for lunch, leave his ashes in a dining hall at a motorway service station. They might not get around to leaving at all, might very well decide to have done with it and tip his dusty remains into the gutter, figuring, perhaps justifiably, that the man to whom these ashes once belonged – or rather, the man whom the ashes, in some other chemical relation, once constituted – is now no longer here, and cannot, therefore, being dead and not in a position to know any different, possibly hold them to account.

He would like, at this point, to say a few words himself on the matter, but for obvious reasons this is simply not possible.

....

Michael Durrant was born in Norwich in 1981.

Meadhbh Ní Eadhra

Ah sure it's grand
Excerpt from a novella

You should see my bedroom. It's plastered in stuff I've wrote up on the walls in different colours, and my space painting, and one of Jade's bras, a purple one, hangin from hooks we put in the ceiling. She's wrote beside it I ran a mini-marathon wearing this in purple marker to match. There's some massive drawings on the wall too, one I done of Bob Marley and then another one of Che Guevara. Jade helped me write up stuff like fear is just a feeling and pure talent bitch and we drew every letter real careful and slow. Me ma nearly had a heart attack when I started decorating me room at first but she's well used to it now and she don't even bother sayin nothin to me about it. Jade said somethin to me a while ago that I knew was gonna be one of the most important things I'd hear, in my whole life, ever, so I wrote it down the side of my wall, where I can see from me bed. It says six billion ways to die but only one way to live. She said she heard it in some rap song but couldn't remember who sang it and I didn't really care anyway so underneath it I wrote by my babi girl jade and put a heart shape next to it to show her how much I love her.

It'd be class to do a graphic design course after school. I don't go round tellin people that I wanna be an artist or anything, cuz they'd think I'm bein a tool, but everyone knows I'm lethal at drawin and even Robbie reckons I could be a famous graffiti artist one day. We were rollin joints the other week and he started drawin a picture of me on one of the pieces of paper and he was gettin it all wrong so I showed him how to do it. He was tryin to draw my cap, and I showed him how there was curves in my cap and he had to keep the curves in if he wanted it to look real. He done it, too, done some nice curves and made it look a lot better than it was before. Jade's not that good at drawing. She says she's not good at writing, either, but she's got this real different way of lookin at things that makes me think she could be a writer if she just learnt some better words and spellin. Sometimes when we're messin about outside or down the skate park or just chillaxin, she says something that makes me stop and be like what did you just say? Cuz she makes so much sense. Cuts through all the shit. Doesn't think past the moment. Like one time we were in a really good mood and pissin ourselves laughin and she came right up to me and whispered in my ear that I was making her lips laugh, and I thought that was really cool and then we started kissin and fuck me, everything was just bloody perfect, d'ya know what I mean? A different night, she told me she couldn't walk home cuz her feet were drunk and I laughed so hard she got kinda mad at me so I stopped but inside I was still laughin and thinkin that no one had ever said that before. Then there's all the stuff nobody else knows about, but it makes me feel sick in my mouth when I think about it, so I wrote a rap song a while ago. It goes like this:

wall broke, all toke, we scope, yu choke,
we bend we mend, come meet my friends,
cause anarky, yu mad at me?
Stop being panicky, yu have only took 3,
don't corner me, cuz i am the cornier,
i warned ya, laughing at silent movies.
Then it's got loads more in the middle and ends like this:
fresh to death,
euphoric pieces of geniusness on my breath,
hummm la di daa,
discribe myself with two words … 'in depth'.

That's the way I've wrote it and it's probly got loadsa mistakes in it but fuckit Jade thought it was rapid so that's good enough for me. I hafta put a proper beat to it but least I got the words down first. Jade said she thinks I'm probly about as good as Tupac or Biggie was when they were our age, like before they went and got famous, and comin from her that's a helluva compliment.

I'm goin smokin with my best pal Robbie tonight. He turned sixteen yesterday and got some money for it so he's after gettin us some weed and we're gonna get baked. I hope he brings Beoga. She's his dalmation and she bounds around like a mad yoke and that's what her name means.

– Karl, your dinner's going cold!

It's me ma. She's been all right to me, so she has. Mosta the time I try to stay out of her way but she's me ma and ya only get one of them so even when she's givin out hell to me she's doin it cuz she wants me to turn out better than most other people we know. I'm gonna get a bitta grub now cuz it'll be a long night and the worst thing is when you're starvin but don't wanna go home in case yer ma don't let ya back out again or in case she cops on to what you're up ta.

*

I stick my cap on, the one I always wear. It's black with flames on it, and I've wrote my initials on the back, in case anyone tries letting on it's theirs. KM. Karl Murray. Looks sorta professional, like the ones some people get specially designed for them when they're in hip hop groups. I'm goin past C&T, our corner shop, now. It's a shitty little place really, but it comes in handy when ya need stuff quick like toilet paper or milk. I drink a pint of milk every day, mostly cuz it tastes gorgeous but I know it's good for your bones too and I like the idea of helping them bones along as much as I can. I'll not have my body strugglin if I can help it. It makes me sick when I see people screwing their bodies up by eating shitloads of takeaways or by eating nothing at all. Why the hell do they do it to themselves? I don't get it. I probly don't have the right to be goin off on one like that cuz I'm goin smokin later, but that's different, isn't it, that's different.

– All ri' Murray? What's the craic?

It's Adam and Mac Dara and the fellas from down the road, sittin on the wall the way they always do, lookin bored as fuck.

– Story?

– Where ya off to? Comin drinkin later?

– Nah, I'm headin to meet Robbie. Where youse plannin on goin tonight, the usual spot?

– Ah gwan outta dat Murray, what ya doin hanging round with yer man Robbie? He's a right retard that youngfella.

Smack. I punch that wanker Gav right in the nose. He thinks he can talk bad bout my mate he's got another think comin. Ah bollix. I should've done that whole countin to ten thing, shouldn't I. Would've saved getting the shit kicked outta me like I know is gonna happen unless I run like fuck away from here. If Jade was here she'd be runnin nowhere, she'd find some way outta this, but then again that girl's bleedin deadly.

Turns out none of them boys can run fast for too long so I get away easy and find Robbie and it's all right again now. Robbie got kicked outta school last year and he's meant ta be goin to Youthreach now, but the waiting list is really long and God knows when they'll get round to his name. Funny thing is, he probly would've gone if there weren't such a long waiting list, cuz it don't sound too bad of a place. Ya get paid every week for turnin up and it's not like school at all, they don't be on at ya the whole time or makin ya do homework or nothin. So it's a pity things worked out the way they did cuz he's got nothin to do and nowhere to be and that's gotta get him down. Here we are anyways, sitting opposite where the old towers used to be, and the both of us sayin nothin to each other, just takin it easy. I remember a few years ago when the last of the seven towers got knocked down, I remember me ma sayin to me it was the end of an era. We used ta live in Clarke Tower, right up on the very top floor. I was twelve when they knocked it down. Everyone said it was about time it got demolished but it was our home for a long time and there's a lot of memories in a place like that. I still find it weird to walk by where the towers used to be and for them all to be gone, vanished into thin air. It don't bother me, or anything, just sayin it's an odd feeling ya get when ya look across the road and see how different everything is now. And even though we got to move to our own gaff with more space round us and not as much stairs to climb, I done a lot of growin up in Clarke Tower and it weren't as bad as people think.

— D'ya know wha some girl called me in town today, Murray?

— Nah, go on.

— A scanger. She called me a bleedin scanger!

— How come?

— Well she seen me nickin a few packs of Taytos in Dunnes and she turns to me and says you're a scanger you, that's all you are. And then she went on and said I bet you're from —

— Bet she had a face like the back of a bus. I'd love to punch the head off her.

— All right all right. Take a chill pill, man, it's grand, everything's grand.

*

The wind's blowin through my jacket and jeans now and hurryin on through Ballymun in that sneaky way of hers. Me and Robbie are smokin a joint round the back of the Reco. Well I'm smokin and he's coughin like an animal. This is a good place to come, cuz it's pretty well hidden but ya can still leg it outta here quickly if ya need to. It's getting proper dark now and Ballymun is changing, turning orange, glowing in the blackness around us. I've never seen street lights being so orange anywhere in the world except for Ballymun, and just cuz I haven't been to very many other places don't mean I can't say that anyway. We're orange tonight, me and Robbie, and right now that's the funniest thing ever and a good enough reason to laugh. It's all just so fuckin funny, the way everyone's turnin orange as they walk by, as if they're bein put in a massive machine and comin out different at the other end. Robbie's trippin out and so am I, but I wanna taste of somethin else. From where I'm standin, ya can see three different roads, and we're right bang in the middle of 'em all. The road on the left goes into town. The one on the right brings ya to Santry and the one straight ahead, right there, that one goes to the M50 and that's the motorway so it'll bring ya anywhere ya wanna go. I'm takin out my pen now and writin on my arm, just to remind myself that I want somethin more than this endless orange sameness night after night after night.

....

Meadhbh Ní Eadhra is from Galway, Ireland. She is this year's winner of The Moth Short Story Prize and the author of two award-winning Irish language books for young people, *Rua* and *Fáinne Fí Fífí*. She is currently working on a novella set in Dublin and a collection of stories set in Belfast city.

Kiare Ladner

Stone Farm
Extract from a novel

On the Cape Coloured side of the village, the roads gained potholes and petered to dust. The air became hazy with smoke, and noisy with Good Hope FM, with chickens and children playing. Here, Freya felt conspicuous, as though her white skin was a fur coat being flaunted. In the faces of the women watching from shaded doorways, she saw contempt: 'we need money; we need work'. She walked faster as she approached Phineas's Vis – but the tin shack was bolted up.

A sign. Go home. Forget it.

'Can we help?'

Some fishermen were hanging around the back, untangling their lines.

'Have you seen Phineas?'

They pointed down to the sea.

'You mean – he's out at sea – on a boat?'

'No madam. He's *mos* in the fokkin sea.'

'Sitting in the blerrie water.'

The fishermen laughed and she laughed with them although she didn't get the joke.

'Come ma'am, I'll take you –'

'Don't worry. I know Phineas.'

She set off in the direction indicated, keeping a steady pace while their laughter swelled. Yet when she reached the beach, it was exactly as they'd said. Phineas was high up, but thigh deep, sitting in the water. The waves came in and a yellow tractor emerged. Aaaah, he was out at sea on his tractor helping to launch a boat. The boat tuc-tuc-tucked towards the horizon and he turned to the shore. He waved animatedly and came over.

'Missus Freya! Long time, no see. *Hoe gaanit?*'

'Good. Well, thank you, "Mister" Phineas.'

'How is that Donnie? Is he over the sickness yet?'

'Getting there.' They walked inland together. 'How're things with you?'

'Hard.' He hoisted his wet trousers up rolling them over at the top. 'Very hard. Not easy. You heard about my boy, the *laat lammetjie,* Jamie?'

'No –'

'He has left.'

'So he isn't helping you anymore?'

He shook his head. 'Not enough work.' He undid a padlock on the door to Phineas's Vis, then lifted the tin flap on the customer's side. He closed himself in behind the counter. Water streamed from his sopping clothes. He put his plastic white fishmonger's apron over them.

'They tell us now we must only fish for this many crayfish a day. So say if you catch more today – then you must put them back. Then you mos hope you catch the buggers again tomorrow! But maybe tomorrow you catch none.'

'What are you going to do?'

'*Wat kan ek doen?*' He raised his hands to the heavens. 'My boy says he will not be told what to do and what not to do like that. He will not work for Donkies.'

'Where's he gone?'

'Cape Town. He thinks he'll live on Gatsbys and champagne. *Jy moenie* generalise *nie* but the kids of today – they have no patience.'

Freya peered into a bucket while Phineas opened his money-tin.

'That's fresh haddock in there,' he said and she nodded. 'But you'll be after some *gaftie* crayfish, *nê?*' He reached into a plastic bucket behind the counter and pulled out a specimen. 'See, still moving.' He gave it a prod. '*Voetsak* hey, old fellow!'

The crayfish edged languidly forward.

'How much each for the crayfish, Phineas?'

'Fifty rand only.'

'I'll have two, then.'

He took three out of the can and set them on the counter.

'For your one hundred, I'll give you a family: mother, father, son.'

'That's very kind of you.'

He nestled the crayfish in a crushed-up Checkers bag and she took three fifties from her pocket. She pressed them into his cold fingers as he looped the handles around her wrist. It was good to have a transaction that enabled each of them to feel generous.

'I hear you're a receptionist now up at the surgery?' He stroked his thumb back and forth across the notes.

'Ja ...'

'And you were selling art before?'

'Just my late husband's. It's almost all gone, Jake's paintings I mean, except for one last piece that I'm not sure I want to sell and some drawings nobody wants because they're very ...' She switched the bag of crayfish to her other wrist. 'I know nothing about art really.'

'Ja, well. Receptionist. That's a proper job. Nice. Well done.'

She looked towards home. 'I'd better be going.'

'Don't leave it so long next time, hey.'

She nodded. On reaching the dirt road, she turned. 'I hope your youngest finds something in Cape Town soon.'

'Thank you, Missus Freya.'

She paused, then waved. He waved back with the notes.

'Very kind of you too,' he added.

She set off at a brisk pace though at the edge of the village, she slowed down. She attempted to move her legs with more grace. Not to jangle the crayfish in their packet, not to hear their rattle as they knocked against each other. Not to imagine their skulls clack-clacking.

Waiting for Donnie in the garden, Freya thrummed her fingers on the table. She'd set it up earlier with a milk bottle of magnolias, a couple of napkins masquerading as placemats and three kitchen candles mounted on saucers. To which she'd added a crayfish stew sizzling in tomato sauce made with fresh herbs and olives, a loaf of crusty farm store bread, two iced cans of Appletizer and a plate toppling with black grapes.

A drop of water plopped between the slats onto her knee. Followed by another, a conjoined one, a double drop. She glanced up at Donnie's window. Behind the flimsy curtains, the filtered sunlight would be fading.

Down here, the Appletizers were dribbling. She put her hand to the stewpot. The cast iron was barely warm.

She got up and crossed the patio.

'Donnie?'

She leaned in through the sliding door.

No reply.

She sighed. An hour had gone by already according to the clock on the wall. She listened to the ticking, allowed the second hand to do a full circle, then went back to the table.

She put a match to one of the candles and watched the wax melt and pool around the wick. From its steady flame, she lit a cigarette.

The chorus of beetles and crickets sang loudly against the wash of the sea. As a child living behind the highway in Pretoria, she used to pretend that the roar of the traffic was the sound of waves, an illusion destroyed only when sirens sliced into it. For so long it had been enough that now, here, there were no sirens. But on an evening like this – she wondered if Donnie had things too easy. All over the country this same sun was going, this same night, coming fast. Most people had so much less; most had suffered loss. What right did they have to think they deserved to be treated differently?

She watched the red clot of sun as it sank below the horizon. Then she ground her cigarette stub into the sand at her feet. Such a sky for such an evening – and Donnie not there to see it.

When the candle had become a cold puddle of wax, he approached the table with an unexpected jauntiness to his step.

'Sitting alone in the dark, Mom?'

'Not at all. I had a party. Tinie Tempah, Driemanskap, Blak Lez, Explicit, who's that other one?

'AKA.'

'Ja her, they all attended. Now they've left.'

'AKA is a him, Mom.'

'Ah, then it wasn't AKA. It was definitely a her.'

'Miss Nthabi maybe?'

'You'll need to show me a picture. Or come down earlier next time.'

'Next time, tell them to wait.'

He served himself a large portion of cold stew and tucked into it hungrily. His volatile nature could be counted on, at any rate. She lit the last two candles and stirred her leftovers around on her plate. When he had finished eating, she put her own knife and fork together.

'It's your birthday soon, Don,' she said. 'Think about what you'd like to get because –'

'Nothing.'

'– sixteen is a biggie and I'd like you to have something special.'

He brushed his index finger through the nearest flame.

'Look, if I'd won the megabucks competition –'

'What?'

He shrugged and she tilted her pack to get at her last smoke.

'Forget it.' He spat on his fingers. Then he closed them over the wicks so that they sizzled. 'No point.'

She scrunched the pack and the cigarette together into a ball.

Nights on the plot were so dense. Odd, how the darkness could be a glittering liberation or an emptiness choked with stars.

She left the table with her fists in her pockets. She strode through the Fynbos and down to the beach. She climbed over the dunes to get to the flat, wet sand where the turtles hatched. This night there were no turtles. She kept going until she reached the outcrop. The expanse of sand shimmered like a stretch of silk behind her spoiled solely by her footprints.

Each time the tension reached a certain level between them, her own adolescent years came flooding back. Had her mother thought she was as close to Freya as Freya assumed she was to her son? Was love for your child, in terms of strength and attachment and intensity, inevitably a one-sided affair? She clambered on, over the black rocks, sharp with shells and slippery with seaweed. At the furthest end there was a heady scent of kelp and mussels exposed by the tide.

She stood there for some time before she sensed that she was no longer alone. A lanky shadow of restlessness was hovering close behind her. Donnie scrambled up and she smiled, despite herself, into the cover of the night.

'Do you reckon I could be an artist, Mom?' he said, joining her.

'You are one.'

'But – like, when I'm finished school – do you think I could earn a living that way? Like Dad did?'

'Why not.'

'With things the way they are now, though, with less money around, even Dad was struggling –'

When he came out with observations she didn't expect, it was like seeing a new wrinkle or freckle in the mirror.

'Sometimes certain styles become less fashionable,' she said.

'But after Dad died, he was in demand again.'

'Perhaps there'd have been a revival if he'd lived.' She looked out at the glow-in-the-dark stoles of foam on the waves that were breaking. 'Shall we head home?'

They crossed the rocks in silence. Then she jumped down to make a spray of sand. 'See, that's why it's worth finishing your schooling, even from home.' She brushed herself off.

'Dad didn't.'

'No, Dad didn't.'

He went ahead of her.

At the edge of the beach, he hung back.

'Mom, about my birthday –'

'Yes?'

'There is something I'd like.'

'What, Donnie?'

His jaw clenched and unclenched, the knobble of bone protruding, retreating, protruding again. She came right up to him and linked her arm through his. As though he'd been just waiting for her to do so, at once he came closer. It was like an odd kind of courtship sometimes between them. She, the older love, accepting her need to make the effort.

They walked along the path, clumsily together, then let go but stayed close.

Back in the kitchen, Freya switched on the light. The fluorescent bulb flickered, then burned strong. Donnie shifted a stack of dishes by the sink. 'I'm going to bed.'

She looked away from him. The window was sticky with sea damp. She wedged it open and the night came in fresh and cool. There was a soft low hoot. She grabbed a torch and shone it into the dark, catching two discs of light.

'Donnie, an eagle owl –'

But, she found he'd left the kitchen – and when she shone the torch again, the owl too had gone.

. . . .

Kiare Ladner's novel *Stone Farm* is the story of a widow's relationship with her son – and of a hit-and-run accident near their home in the Western Cape. Her next project takes the more comic, oblique slant of her short stories. She received the David Higham Award in 2012.

Jess Lowry

The Thaw

I t was March and the storm moved in quickly. And because it was lambing season and because Faustus Smith had, months ago, put away the snowplough and the basher and the groomer – the weather caught the Hillsborough farm off guard. The flocks from the outer field were still being counted in as the first flakes began to fall. A hundred sheep – half the flock – were missing.

Faustus, his farmhands knew, was always careful about snow. The farmer made it his business to know when the winds were changing, got the animals in quickly and sent his employees home early with instructions to drive safely. As a result, Faustus hadn't lost a single animal to a drift in his 62 years. But now – instead of falling – the spring snow was flying sidewise and sudden. Not signalled by the slow curdling of clouds all day and a flake or two drifting downward, but rushing forward all at once as though sent for. The blue sky was gone and nobody had a jacket. Informed that half the flock was missing and the worst of storm was only miles away, Faustus grabbed his most experienced farmhand and instructed him to drive to the outer fields in the blue truck.

Together Faustus and his farmhand toured the base of the hill and drove up the steep paths to the side of the pasture. The grass which only that afternoon had been enjoying sun – prickled up through its new white nightdress. In its sharp, green points – it froze on end in astonishment. Faustus sent his dog into the outer pastures but it returned alone, its bark echoing into the wind. The collie's white fur blended with the backdrop making it look like only half an animal was slouching towards them – one shoulder rising above the other. As the sun began to set, the snow was coming faster and the farmhand – leaning close to the windscreen – said he would barely be able to see his way through the crossings soon. They should, he said, return to the farm. The sheep would last the night. 'Cold won't kill them,' he said. 'It's hunger they die of.' Faustus said nothing.

His dinner growing cold on the kitchen table, the farmer watched out the window as the flakes fell. He thought of the sheep – out there somewhere in the cold. Standing together under a tree or in a dale watching the same flakes with their wide, black eyes. The drifts would be rising by now, he thought, covering the long grass and the fences – the buses and the small trees. 'A hundred sheep,' his wife said as she moved her water glass between her palms. 'How could a hundred sheep go missing?' To her husband's silence, she turned up the television as a grim weather forecaster in a pink blouse and yellow skirt on the *8 O'clock News* placed little white clouds over most of the country. The channel flashed between reporters in different parts of the country who stood with their hands covering their ears or holding onto a tree. 'Gale force,' one said. 'Freak storm,' said another. His wife cleared away Faustus's full plate before going to bed calling goodnight to Faustus who kept his vigil by the window.

As he watched the whiting out of the outside world – all the snows of Faustus's life fell before his eyes. He was a boy on a silver tray – sledding down the hill in Somerset – the silver burning through his mittens. He was falling out of a pub into the cold with Rose McDermott whose hair was soft under his fingers He was driving towards the hospital the night his son was born.

Faustus had been in Dorset that night and had received the phone call that his son was entering the world. The baby, the doctor he spoke to explained, was two months early and too small. It was February and Faustus set out at midnight – driving an old, brown car towards where his wife had been staying with her mother. The journey was three hours and he kept the windows down as the increasingly white world whipped past him – the flakes burning his eyes. He had been driving too fast when he hit the deer. By the sounds of it, a big deer.

'A big deer,' he told his wife three weeks later as they bundled the baby into the car and she looked at the dent on the fender.

He watched from the window now as the snow filled up the world's concavities, pillowing up in the gloaming, making night light with its whiteness, and then falling still, he imagined, in every one's dreams, falling for pages and pages.

Dawn revealed the snow was endless, a heavy blanket on the outdoors. Rivers, fields, trees, and roads had disappeared and the landscape had become white mounds and hollows. It was hard to see where earth merged with the sky and the horizon stretched on into a footprintless world.

At first light, Faustus set off with more men and with more dogs. The roads that had been clear the day before were no longer visible. The search party moved in a pack with provisions of hot tea and rounds of sandwiches, bottles of water and packets of shortbread. They carried ropes and spades and forks and sand and feed and wire and radios. They brought only the biggest dogs and watched them scramble up the dales out in front – their black coats glistening against the snow as they made white canyons with their muzzles on the ground.

They found a half-buried tractor. Abandoned cars. A dead pig. And seven sheep from a nearby village. The animals were too cold to bleat and swayed on the spot as the party approached. Two men volunteered to take them back to the farm whose insignia was sprayed on their icy wool. But the farmer kept going – forging on into the white world. They tripped over branches that'd fallen – reaching out from the ground like laced fingers. Faustus put his boot through thin ice that had glossed the lake and didn't remove it until another party pulled him back, cold shooting up through his veins until the farmer imagined his eyes lasering out blue beams into the stillness.

The party climbed over stiles and fences and dug away at air-pockets in the hope of finding the flock. They spoke to other groups they came across who all shook their heads: 'A hundred sheep?' They ran out of supplies after six hours and, by the afternoon, the snow started again. Faster this time. Rubber boots began to slide on the ice as the ground began to freeze under their feet. The trees shivered and all the birds went silent as the world braced for its white nightgown.

'We have to go back,' the farmer's daughter-in-law said – wiping her eyes that were streaming in the wind. 'We have to go back.' And so they turned back – taking the farmer with them.

Back in the farmhouse, the search party stood around the kitchen and drank thick soup from mugs. They rubbed their hands together and blew on their knuckles as the drift rose outside. The farmer's son did the calculation of the lost sheep. 'Snow cost' he muttered to his wife as she pressed tea into his hands. The losses, he said quietly, pushing the paper towards the farmer, would be severe. 'Recoverable,' he said. 'But harsh. I'll call the bank tomorrow.' Faustus didn't move from the window and didn't take his hands from his pockets where they had stayed – frostbitten – since his return. He said nothing when the group bade him goodnight. Sorry for his troubles, they called that they would, perhaps, have better luck tomorrow. The weather might change his son said, standing behind Faustus so that his reflection was amongst the snow: 'We could get lucky.'

Those who could walk home made their way out into the storm. Pulling their hats and scarfs around their mouths, their last words as they headed out into the night were muffled or whipped away by the wind and heard only by the sheep who were still out there, somewhere, in the cold. Those whose cars were trapped in the yard were shown to spare rooms by the farmer's wife. 'Come to bed, Faustus,' she said, as the last of that night's guest were dispatched. 'There's nothing you can do now.'

'In a minute,' the farmer said, rocking back on his heels but not turning around. 'I'll be there in a minute.'

The moment before impact, he had seen the shadow to the right of his window screen. And heard it fall. With a thud. On the snow. Outside the door. The wind, he told himself, it moaned at that precise moment and a bird from the forest called out though it was unlike any bird he had heard then or since.

His heartbeat had been in his hands. The steering wheel pulsed as Faustus had removed the key from the ignition. The world went dark without his headlights and there was only the sound of the snow falling. And another cry from the strange bird. And a moan from the wind though the trees were still. The window-wipers – paused on the windscreen – accumulated a drift in diagonal and cut the outside world in half. Faustus opened his car door and steadied himself to see the deer. For it was a deer, he thought. It had to be a deer. But he paused as the flakes entered the light from the car. They spun in place – momentarily yellow – before they fell and melted or melted and fell: Faustus couldn't tell which came first. It was such a waste, he thought, as the crystals died in the light. It was such a waste of intricate beauty. Their life had been so short.

The car door chimed to mind him it was open. But the world was otherwise still. And quiet. The deer, he surmised, was dead. There was no one else on the road. 'It was a deer,' Faustus said out loud and to the car. 'It was only a deer.'

He shut the door and the chime from the consul stopped. The engine boomed through the surrounding clearings and the lights once more illuminated the road in front and the mounting banks of ice to his left and right. Closing his eyes, Faustus pressed his foot on the accelerator and moved forward. His wheels passed over something large beneath – an unseen bump and crunch. Gripping the steering wheel, Faustus drove on. He didn't stop until he reached the hospital and had never looked back.

And now he stood at the window and wondered how the sheep had wandered so far.

It snowed all week. Wheels and footsteps moved soundlessly on the street, as if the business of living continued secretly behind a pale but impenetrable curtain. In the falling quiet there was no sky or earth, only snow lifting in the wind, frosting the window glass, chilling the rooms, deadening and hushing the nearby city. Faustus lost track of the days: Friday was no different from Saturday. The council dropped feed over the frosted hills and there was hope, within the community, that sheep would be pulled alive. But Faustus – looking out over the land – knew there was no hope.

When the thaw came the sheep were found. They were over the side of the hill and pushed in against a ridge. Some had continued upward and died. Some went downward and died. Some stayed where they were. They died as well. Pulled black like a cotton blanket – the melt revealed the creatures with their eyes half-open and their lips frosted shut. Their wool was dark from the mud and their irises were milky and wide at something the farmhands loading them into the trucks couldn't see.

It was dark when Faustus loaded the last sheep – slinging the beast over his shoulder – he walked into the oncoming night.

. . . .

Jess Lowry is a Master's student on the Prose Fiction course at UEA. She writes short fiction and is working on a collection of stories.

Matthew McGuinness

The Skin on the Bear
An excerpt

'**B**y the shrine. Here. Here,' said Grabowski, jabbing his finger at a little stone grotto coming up fast by the side of the road.

Urbaniak braked at the last moment and turned the patrol car onto the forest track. An eighteen-wheeler from Ukraine that had been riding up their arses all the way from Jarocin went barrelling past and blasted them with its horn. Grabowski twisted in his seat and muttered into his moustache.

'Fucking chadziajs.'

Urbaniak crossed himself airily on account of the statue sheltering in the grotto.

The car juddered violently as they motored over the frozen mud surface of the track, passing down a straight tunnel of leafless ash trees and silver birch.

'Krawiec! Hoy, Krawiec,' shouted Urbaniak over the wheel noise, glancing into his rear-view mirror. A skinny man-boy lounged on the back seat wearing an Aquascutum baseball cap – Jarocin town council's contractor for seizures and car removals. He leaned forward, tapping a diamond-studded ear. Urbaniak raised his voice a notch. 'You met this guy before? This Olenski?'

Krawiec shrugged. 'Me and Stef went there for small stuff – TVs and computers. Didn't find any.'

'Did you see any firearms in the house? Or knives?'

'Jesus Maria, don't wet yourself,' said Grabowski. 'There's no gun licence at the address.'

'You can never be sure with country boys,' said Urbaniak, but his partner just shook his head and turned to stare out of the window.

Grabowski wasn't himself – hadn't been for a couple of days. His usual stream of bile had more or less dried up. The change had come about on Tuesday during a visit to his regular night-duty fuck. Urbaniak had been surprised to see his partner emerge from the apartment block after only about ten minutes with a face on him like a Tatar's arse. Best not to probe, he had concluded – beware of unexploded bombs.

Urbaniak let the question of firearms slide too. He shouted over his shoulder at Krawiec instead: 'So how did Olenski take it? A couple of bailiffs turning up I mean. Did he threaten you?'

'Threaten? Me? That's funny. Very funny,' said Krawiec.

Urbaniak continued to watch the young man in the rear-view mirror.

'Threatened?' Krawiec continued. 'I don't know how you can even say that. You'd need a diamond drill to get through this toughened exterior, officer my man.'

Grabowski snorted. 'You'd be pissing your baggy-arsed jeans if you had to police a cup tie.'

'OK, big man,' said Krawiec. 'You just give it your best shot with Olenski,' and he leaned back in his seat.

'What do you mean?' asked Urbaniak. But the conversation was apparently over. Krawiec was working the whole gangster thing – his legs and arms spread wide, nodding along to a beat in his head.

They crossed a boggy frozen stream, rattling over a plank bridge, and a little further on emerged into a clearing – the end of the road. On the far side of the open space there was a row of four cottages – brick-built, with upper floors made of dark grainy timber. Spread out over the greater part of the clearing was a jumbled assembly of fridges, bed frames, tyres, bathroom suites, prams, radiators and all the other bits of junk that Franek Olenski had scrounged over the years. He was a familiar figure in the villages, towing a loaded trailer behind his rusty Polonez – peering over fences.

Urbaniak drove slowly round the edge of the dump and parked by the cottages. Climbing out, he gave a complicated whistle of amazement.

'I know man. Must be worth thousands in scrap value,' said Krawiec. He slammed the car door and the noise clattered around the forest, causing a woodpecker to leave off hammering momentarily. 'I told them at the court. I said they should just take this.'

'Health risk?' speculated Urbaniak.

Krawiec shook his head: 'I'd turn this into liquid assets in twenty-four hours. No problem.'

'Did you remember your kit?' sighed Grabowski, zipping up his winter coat on the other side of the car. Krawiec produced a leather tool roll from the pocket of his oversize parka and waved it aloft. Grabowski continued wearily: 'Right. It doesn't look like our man is here. At least his car isn't. So, Urbaniak, you can knock up the first set of neighbours and I'll do the second. Ask if they know when he's going to be back. And you,' he said, addressing Krawiec, 'just stay put.'

A tabby cat – a long-legged huntress – had sidled out from among the junk and Krawiec was already busy making friends with it.

Urbaniak rattled the gate of the first cottage. No dog came. He went round to the back of the house and saw an Alsatian with a patchy coat chained to a stake. It was shivering on the ground among its own turds. It stood up without barking.

Someone was obviously at home in the cottage. Heavy yellow smoke was spilling out of the chimney. The back door was open so Urbaniak walked in. Standing in an unlit hallway he called out several times and eventually footsteps were heard, slow and heavy, rising up some basement stairs. A man emerged from a door on the left and flicked a light switch. A bare overhead bulb came on. The man was about thirty – unshaven with red-rimmed, evasive eyes.

'Sorry. I was seeing to the boiler,' he said in a vague, faraway voice. He stripped off a pair of dirty latex gloves but didn't offer his hand.

'Officer Urbaniak from Jarocin. Sorry to intrude.'

The man ignored the presented ID.

'Bednarek. You're looking for Franek I suppose.'

'Yes sir, we are. Do you know when ...'

'He's not around.'

'When will Mister Olenski be back?'

'How should I know? He's a free man.'

'When does he usually come back?'

'He does as he pleases. I'm not his mother.'

Urbaniak took a deep breath and regrouped.

The name Bednarek was familiar. The original complainant maybe? Yes. The neighbour who petitioned the court to get Olenski's junk taken away.

'How have things been between you and Olenski?' he asked. 'Since the court decision?'

Bednarek didn't answer. He stared down at his hands, which were twisting and stretching the latex gloves.

'Has he threatened you in any way?'

No answer.

'I expect he was a bit annoyed to be fined wasn't he?'

Bednarek threw the gloves aside. 'Listen to me,' he said, spitting out the words, but in an undertone as if someone were sleeping in the next room. 'I don't know why you think you have to chase Franek and plague him and make his life a misery. It's nothing to do with me. Fining him! What good is that going to do anyone?' His red-rimmed eyes were no longer evasive; they were narrow and scornful.

Urbaniak glanced over his shoulder towards the door. 'Well, isn't that a bit ungrateful?' he said. 'I mean, I don't know all the details, but the court did tell Olenski to clear away his rubbish, and that's what you wanted, right? He obviously hasn't complied, so they had to fine him really. It's just their procedure.'

Bednarek now had his arms crossed tightly as if to restrain himself, and stood staring at the floor, breathing heavily.

Urbaniak continued: 'He didn't even pay the fine. That's why we've come – to take his car away. We're on your side, you see?'

'Oh Jesus,' said Bednarek. 'You're taking his car now? God, forgive me. I just wanted the rubbish removed, that's all. How's the man going to live without a car?'

'What do you care?' said Urbaniak with a shrug. 'Look at the state of that area out front. There's probably battery acid and all sorts running off it into your well. That animal deserves everything he gets.'

Bednarek screwed his fists up, and Urbaniak popped the stud on his baton holder. There was silence for a few seconds.

'Come in,' said Bednarek coldly. 'Let me show you something.'

They went through into the main part of the house – Urbaniak hanging back just a little. There was one room for living and sleeping, with a large pull-out sofa bed and a cot next to it. A glass coffee table was covered with dirty cups and plates, and an old cathode-ray tube TV was showing a computer game paused in mid-shootout. The place smelled of farts.

Bednarek snatched his phone from the windowsill and positioned himself next to Urbaniak. He began thumbing through pictures on the screen and showing them one by one. In the first there was a chubby-legged girl of about three, naked, sitting in a paddling pool. The Alsatian was in the background drinking from the water. Next one: the same child pedalling a tricycle, open-mouthed, probably squealing. Old car tyres had been laid out to make a race track for her. Next: a close-up of the girl, aged about five now, cuddling a more clean-cut version of Bednarek and wearing a pink crocheted skull-cap.

Something was happening out in front of the house. Urbaniak could hear raised voices, but it would be disrespectful to look away from the photos. He shut out the sound instead.

In the next picture the girl was lying in a bare white cot, hugging a teddy bear and making the same open-mouthed squealy face, but now she only had wisps of hair, and smooth ridges where her eyebrows should have been.

'Leukemia,' said Bednarek in a matter-of-fact tone, as if he were saying the girl's name. 'She's in the special unit over at Poznań, due to have her second lot of chemo.'

'I'm sorry. I hope everything works out for you. What are the doctors saying?'

'My wife's there. She deals with all that.'

'She sends the pictures does she? Keeps you updated?'

'It was her who blamed the cancer on Franek's rubbish. Just what you said – claimed he'd poisoned the water. So because of that she convinced the doctors or social workers or whatever to let them stay full time, sleeping together in a room at the hospital. I didn't think she was right about the rubbish, but I wrote to the court anyway –

asked them to get it taken away. I'd have done anything just to get my kid home, at least between chemo sessions. I just wanted to be a family again. But then she told me – my wife. She said it didn't really matter what the court said or what happened with the rubbish. She wasn't ever coming home. Whether our daughter lived or died, that was the end for us. She got a court order – banned me from the hospital.'

Bednarek paused on a picture of the girl with a yellow complexion, wired up to cannulas and computers in hospital. She was glancing over the top of her Gameboy, looking distinctly annoyed at the intrusion.

Urbaniak hardly knew what to say. It was obvious now why Bednarek had come on so hostile earlier. He'd summoned up devils – the courts and the police – and now there was no way of exorcising them. Reporting your neighbour really was the one unforgiveable sin in a village, let alone a tiny hamlet like this. Bednarek would live to regret it for sure.

The clamour of voices started up outside again. Urbaniak went over to the window and pulled aside the dirty lace curtain. A Polonez saloon from the eighties – brush-painted in dark green – had been parked behind the patrol car. Krawiec was kneeling next to the driver's side working at the lock, and Grabowski was standing guard over him, baton in hand. A third man was squaring up to them. He was short, with bowed legs – dressed in blue dungarees over at least two sweaters. Between fits of arm-waving and shouting he rocked from foot to foot. It was Olenski.

Matthew McGuinness is currently finishing his first novel – a police procedural. Born in the badlands of South London towards the end of the sixties, Matthew took up novel writing after a couple of decades spent buried alive.

Rachel Mendel

Soap

Extract from a novel

Beaux's monologue provides comfortable background noise, like a familiar record played on vinyl, as I critique my various wardrobe options. My lipstick and eye shadow are already perfect – I don't like doing my make-up in front of other women, and nor does Beaux. It's a female secret, the process of transforming one's face. I don't think I've ever seen her without at least mascara and foundation on. In an opener moment, she admitted to me that when she'd been going out with Damian, her one long-term relationship, she used to sneak out of bed at six in the morning to do her eyes so that she could 'wake up' at eight with him, looking as prettily perfect as a fairytale princess. That's Beaux for you – her looks are everything to her, simply because no one's ever bothered to appreciate her for anything else.

I've tried to explain to her that some men are attracted to the way you look, and some are just attracted to you – you can't win the former and you can't lose the latter, no matter how bad you look first thing in the morning with a hangover. But Beaux is younger than me, and used to hanging around with the wrong kind of women: girls with breast implants and six-month-old babies, girls with fake nails which they don't draw in, girls who fight each other in The Regal on a Saturday night because their boyfriends have been two-timing them, while the pock-marked studs film the hair-pulling on their mobile phones and go home with the victors. Accordingly, I don't think she quite trusts me yet, despite our three-year friendship – even though I live with her, every time I see her it's like starting at the beginning: breaking her down until she stops the female jousting and we can have a decent conversation.

She's feeling threatened right now, so the claws are out – it's not that she isn't rooting for me exactly, it's just that her perception is clouded by how tonight might affect her. What if Mikah likes me enough to offer me a new life, which Beaux isn't a part of? Not to mention that, for girls like Beaux, any woman around her getting into a relationship is a blow to her ego. She's obviously trying to connect with me by asking my advice, but can't help attempting to assert her superiority over me: her anxieties are couched by boasts about free five-course meals, and Ollie's flattering, but regrettable, *keenness*. I can feel her words start to penetrate my bubble of anticipation: she's drawing me in, despite myself. So I drop the stocking I'd been scrabbling to find a partner for, and, spinning around, offer her the most pertinent bit of advice which I can impart upon a younger woman at this point in my sexual journey:

'Never fuck anyone whose arsehole you wouldn't lick. That's my moral code when it comes to sex. And it's seriously the deepest and best advice which I can give you. Think about it –'

'That's completely disgusting, Lily. I'm not going to lick his arsehole. We're not even going out.'

'You're misunderstanding me. I'm qualifying the morality behind you sleeping with this guy, not telling you how to do it. What I'm saying is –'

'What you're saying is that it's immoral for me to sleep with Ollie?'

'I'm not saying that at all. You asked if you're at the point where you ought to sleep with him. You asked if, considering your ambiguity towards him, that would make you a slag. I'm saying, no, not necessarily – not as long as theoretically, and only theoretically mind, you would voluntarily lick his arsehole.'

Beaux looks quite upset by this apparent inversion of common sense.

'Right, so by your logic, I'm a slut and I haven't even slept with him yet, whereas Christine Moranson and her brigade of anal fisting boyfriends are basically the Twelve Disciples of the Apostle.'

'I'm not saying that at all. It's a question of personal choice. And of standards. You remember Andrew, right? That Canadian guy I was seeing in first year. OK, so you know what he was like about women

– told me straight up the second time I met him that he wouldn't fuck a woman if she had a single hair on her body apart from on her head. Wouldn't go down on me even though I complied. Yeah? Squeamish, selfish or immature, whatever you wanna call it. OK, so we're hung over on the tube to Borough to get a fry-up at the only place Andrew deemed worthy, even though it's fucking miles away – you know what he was like. And we see this little girl – I swear she must've been fourteen – she'd got these jeans on, right, the kind so tight she'd probably be three inches shorter if she took them off, and one of those clip-on blonde ponytails where there's this like, tuft of chopped hair sticking out either side of it where the real hair ends – totally gross, but she had a hard little body on her – Andrew was a complete fucking paedophile anyway – he goes, just sort of under his breath, like he'd forgotten I was there: Man I would totally lick that girl's asshole. And then again: I would so lick that girl's asshole.'

Beaux looks momentarily nonplussed, before responding exactly how I'd expected her to.

'What a creep. You know, I always thought he was weird. Whenever I came into the kitchen when you guys were here he'd always look at me in my shorts ...'

'Yeah yeah. That's not the point. The point was, he'd look at other girls all the time, right, but what he said then – that actually upset me. I didn't say anything – I was all grotty and hung over, and what he'd said had embarrassed me, somehow, I didn't want to look at him – no, I didn't want him to look at me – so I just sat opposite him along one of those bright exposed benches in Dixon's Cottage and let him eat my mushrooms and sausages and thought about how he never, ever kissed me in public and how once I texted him this drunk picture of myself in lingerie and he never even texted me back –'

'You never told me that – you always said he was sweet with you, that he was a bit damaged –'

'It was complicated. He was a very intelligent alcoholic and he'd just come out of a serious relationship. And it wasn't as if I actually liked him as a person. He was a massive drag. Do you remember the way he used to go on about things? "I've fucked this and I've snorted that and sold them and lived there and been places, man", and he seemed so old the way he went on about being a teenager in fucking Canada all the time. His voice, his body, his tattoo – those were the only reasons I went out with him.'

'Yeah, I remember you saying that at the time. You're forgetting something else –'

'That comes under "body".'

We laugh briefly, and then Beaux puts her innocent face back on.

'Still, I can't believe you never told me any of this at the time. I thought he really, you know, *liked* you.'

The obviousness of its execution renders her attack harmless, almost cute, like she's a child mimicking her mother's voice. She's using my nail scissors to cut her split ends onto my bed – I watch as she isolates a single hair and snips it contemptuously, as though brushing away a beggar's hand. I pass her a piece of newspaper to cut onto, which she looks at blankly and then places on my dresser.

'I have my pride. Imagine if your boyfriend said he'd lick some other girl's arsehole when he's never even licked yours. It's pretty terrible, isn't it?'

Beaux looks at me, and I can tell she's wondering what's wrong with my arsehole.

'I guess. Not that I'd let anyone anywhere near my … you know.'

'Why not if they wanted to? And anyway, you're still not getting my point. The point is, I went home and thought about it, and I realised I would lick Andrew's arsehole. I'd got near it when I was sucking his dick, obviously, and it smelled like it was on fucking fire. And I'd still have licked it if he'd really wanted me to. I fancied him that much.'

I'm half joking, but Beaux is looking sorry for me in a way which tries the limits of my patience. She has to remember that I am speaking from the morally impeachable stance of someone who is in love, while she is only seeing Ollie out of the need for constant reassurance that she is beautiful, as well as a few nice dinners and the illusion of having a friend. I push on.

'Licking arsehole – that's the kind of attraction which goes beyond logic or disgust, the kind of attraction that makes you really engage with your partner physically. I hadn't meant to lock in to Andrew chemically like that. So that was when I realised that he must have just been using me for sex. I thought about the guys who've been really crazy about me, and they've always been drawn towards my arsehole at some point – going a bit south when they're eating you out, a bit north when you're doing it doggy style, or getting a bit over-enthusiastic with their fingers. You know what I mean?'

Beaux's face is straining with the effort of demonstrating that she has precisely no idea what I mean, and nor does she want to. I don't wait for her response.

'Don't look at me like that, you know exactly what I'm talking about, you're not a *virgin*. Fuck, when I was going out with Elliot, he was always trying to get his hand down there for a "laugh" – he picked me up from work one time – I'd been walking about all day in the fucking Indoor Plants section working up a sweat, and when he hugged me hello he slipped his fingers right the way down my arse-crack – Jesus, I was so embarrassed – and I caught him *smelling his fingers afterwards.* Face it, your arse is your chemical essence, it's the hole which leads to your soul. I think to really fancy you, to really want *you*, a guy needs to have that level of attraction. Andrew just wanted to fuck me, he didn't want to connect. And I'd suddenly realised that my body was trying to connect with him, against my will. That was why I really broke up with him.'

'Because you started to have feelings and he wasn't interested?'

'No. Because I'd have licked his arsehole and he'd probably have broken up with me for asking him to lick mine. And I didn't have feelings, I had disproportionately wet underpants.'

Beaux fishes a Dior lipstick up from the clutter on my desk, applies it with an expression of intense self-love and smacks her lips together disapprovingly.

'I still don't see what this has to do with me and Ollie … he's obviously crazy about me and I'm sure he'd do that, *if* I wanted him to, which I *don't.'*

I'm growing tired of this conversation.

'Ollie obviously would lick your arsehole. You obviously wouldn't lick his. Which means you're lowering yourself if you have sex with him because you don't really fancy him, and what's worse is you're using him, because you know how much he likes you. That is my point.'

'Using him for what?'

There's a pause where neither of us says the obvious, before Beaux speaks again.

'Would you lick Mikah's arsehole?'

A beatific smile spreads across my face.

'Beaux, I would bend that guy over and eat him out with a spoon.'

Rachel Mendel was born in Halifax, Nova Scotia, and has lived in various countries including Nigeria and Turkey. She completed her BA in English at Loughborough University, and works as a freelance copywriter when she's not working on her novel.

Thomas Morris

Low

I helped them move in. It was June and I could feel the sweat on my back trickling down under the waistband of my boxers, down to the crack of my arse. They seemed a good couple, but he was annoying, a bit too serious about himself − like he'd always wear a collared shirt, no matter the weather. He told me he worked at the Miners' Hospital doing X-rays and that she wrote music reviews. I think he wanted me to be impressed by their maturity. When we carried in the big couch, Emma trailed behind us with a cat in a white cage. She let it out in the living room and it edged its way around the walls then rubbed up against me.

'That's strange,' Emma said, 'she usually doesn't like men.'

Paul looked jealous, as if I'd somehow planned the whole thing.

'I'm gonna go and pick up the rest of the stuff,' he said. 'You coming?'

Emma said no, that she'd rather stay and sort things out. He gave her a kiss on the cheek, then left.

'Any chance of a coffee?' Emma said to me.

'Aye,' I said, and took her next door to mine.

I boiled the kettle and she sat cross-legged on the carpet inspecting my CD collection. I stole occasional glances to see if any of it impressed her. She coiled her hair around a finger.

'Who you writing reviews for then?' I asked.

'Oh, I don't really write them for anyone,' she said. 'That's just something Paul tells people.'

I nodded.

'Well I try to write them,' she said. 'You've odd taste in music, by the way.'

'It's eclectic,' I said.

She took out a CD, studied the back of the case. 'I think I'd call it manic.'

She told me she didn't take milk on account of her dodgy stomach, and when I gave her the coffee, she took it to the sink and added cold water.

We took our drinks through to her place and she showed me the holes in the landing wall. They'd been Polyfilla'd over, but it still looked like someone had taken a golf club to it.

'What were the last lot like?' she said, her leg shaking on the spot. 'The ones who lived here, I mean.'

'Oh, you know . . . peaceful,' I said. 'The kind of people who settle arguments with sports equipment.'

She blew on her coffee. 'I used to keep a cricket bat next to my bed,' she said. 'When I was young.'

'When you were young?' I said. 'What, like a fetus?'

She smiled. 'How old are you then?'

I told her I was thirty-four. She told me she was twenty-six, and asked how people my age spent their time.

'A good question,' I said. 'I'll have to get back to you on it.'

'Yeah well,' she said, 'you know where I live.'

That evening I took them to the Courthouse for a welcome-to-the-area pint. It was hot inside – the place was crowded with guys in cut-off vests bulging with red skin, and girls lathered in fake tan. Emma and Paul were tired and crabby, and the conversation was tough. Paul took slow sips of his pint and looked around the bar, while Emma reached into her drink and pulled out the ice cubes, placing them on the table. When she left for the toilet, Paul touched me on the shoulder.

'Well, thanks for all your help today,' he said.

'No worries,' I said, and looked at the small ice puddles on the table. I think I only met him once after that.

I felt as if I'd been a bit overly-friendly, so I didn't have much to do with them the next few weeks. I went back to applying for jobs and going for walks. I was at a low ebb. I'd found pinworms in my stools, thin white things curling and uncurling in my shit in the toilet. And while I knew which tablets to get – I'd had worms before – I couldn't face going to the pharmacy. So I tried just to shower every day, to wash my bed sheets every week. It didn't really work though. I still found myself scratching at night, and then having to get up to clean under my fingernails before trying to go back to sleep.

But I barely slept then. I'd stay up till three or four in the morning watching documentaries and crap subtitled films about prostitutes, civil wars and parents with Alzheimer's. I'd sleep through until twelve or one the next day, and then go to Glanmors for a pasty and a custard slice. And I was doing my usual breakfast trip when I ran into Emma again. She was coming out of Tesco, shopping bags looped over her arms, a wooden necklace swinging. We walked back home together through the lanes. There was the rattle of wheels on the pavement, as parents pushed empty pushchairs to pick up their kids from the nursery. Emma said she found the empty prams creepy. She didn't like how happy the parents looked.

When we got back to hers she gave me a plate for my pasty, and started going on about being a kid.

'My mother was French and crazy,' she said, twirling and untwirling the hair at the back of her head. 'The two don't necessarily go together but –'

'Yeah,' I said, taking a bite. The corned beef filling burned the roof of my mouth a little.

'She was really weird about food too, really strict. She'd only ever give me protein shakes and it messed up my stomach. I think that's what gave me IBS.'

'Shit,' I said. I watched the cat jump up onto the couch.

'Yeah,' she said, and stroked the cat. She went to twiddle its fur but the cat moved off the couch and came over to me, brushing its body against my leg.

Emma watched, then stretched out her arms, as if in a yawn, and massaged her neck.

'Mind if I do some stretches?'

'It's your house,' I said. And she got down on the carpet and did a few yoga poses. I took a bite of my pasty and watched.

We began to hang out a lot after that. I'd go over in the afternoons, under the guise of helping her paint the living room or the kitchen, and we'd spend most of the time just talking. In one week she told me that musicians should be paid by the state, that there wasn't enough evidence to support global warming, and that her boyfriend liked it when she wore masks during sex.

'What kind of masks?' I said.

'Celebrities,' she said. 'Actors mainly.'

I asked her where they got the masks from, but she just laughed.

Those afternoons when we sat in her living room and she'd have her hair down, all casual, and her tanned neck would be gracefully there, moving as her head bobbed to whatever music we were listening to – it all felt like the last day of a sickness, when you're over the worst, but take one more day off and it's glorious. At one point the agency called and said they had work for me – I just had to turn up to the site on the Wednesday and the job was mine.

But I'm glad I didn't go. Because that Wednesday, when I went around to hers, she started crying on the couch for no reason. I went to give her a hug but she lifted her head and kissed me on the lips. I said we shouldn't, but she nodded then kissed me again, climbing on top of me. Her skin was tanned. And when I lifted the cup of the bra, her breasts were pale.

She asked me if I wanted her to wear a mask. I told her no.

'Please,' she said.

'All right then,' I said.

She went to the bedroom and came back wearing a Natalie Portman mask. She climbed back on top of me, and pushed me inside her. And all the time I was torn between wanting to look at her and needing to look away. I was afraid it'd be over too soon if I watched her arched neck, or listened too intently. And I was afraid to change position in case she touched my bum, in case the worms were out and wriggling. But none of that happened. I held her firmly and she grinded against me, and all the while the cat looked on from the carpet. When we finished, we lay on the couch – my head on her chest – and she tousled my hair. We even fell asleep. When we woke, all she said was:

'Do you want a cuppa tea?'

After I left I went to the pharmacist on Cardiff Road and bought a box of Vermox. The woman at the till didn't bother looking to see what it was, she just scanned it through, and put it in a bag.

I felt a small charge in me the rest of the evening, like something was rattling in the blood. The next day, Emma came over to mine and I brushed her hair behind her ear, kissed her on the neck. She pulled away.

'No offence,' she said, 'but yesterday just didn't feel good. Nothing against you. You know how sometimes it just isn't there between two people?'

'How do you mean?'

'You know,' she said, her hand going to her hair again, 'when it's just not there, the connection or whatever you wanna call it.'

'Oh right,' I said. 'Yeah, I think I felt the same.'

That night I moved my bed against the wall, to be closer to her. When they had sex, I'd put my ear right next to it, and sometimes I touched myself and sometimes I'd just be tormented by it all.

We still saw each other though. If anything, I got to know her better. She talked a lot, mostly about her mum. And she'd give me presents too: books, DVDs, and even some mix CDs that she made especially for me. She titled one of them 'Music School Dropout'. I still listen to it sometimes.

Towards the end of July, when the nursery broke up for summer, and the empty pushchairs stopped rolling by my window, I went round to Emma's. She was sat on the floor, doing a jigsaw she'd bought at a charity shop. It was detective-themed. There was a booklet that went along with it which contained a short story: a murder mystery. The key clue was in the completed jigsaw, and there was no picture on the box. Emma seemed quiet. Her leg was shaking again.

I told her how my father, during a low spell, had once cut the pieces of a jigsaw with scissors to 'make them fit'.

'I think I might be pregnant,' she said. And she tapped a jigsaw piece on the carpet floor.

I thought of my sperm rushing inside her.

'I'm not keeping it,' she said.

'Is it –'

'It's his,' she said.

She kept the baby – a little girl they named Natalie. The place was too small for the kid, so they moved to a semi in Castle View a few weeks before it was born. I see Emma quite a bit – in Tesco, down by the castle, outside Glanmors – she always stops for a chat, but we don't have that much to talk about.

And every few months, the worms come back. Apparently they lay their eggs at night.

Thomas Morris is from Caerphilly, South Wales. He is currently working on two projects: a collection of short stories set in Caerphilly, and a tragicomic novel, *Second Best: The Diaries of a Substitute Goalkeeper*. He is Assistant Editor at The Stinging Fly – a small, Dublin-based press. Email: tolmorris@gmail.com.

Lisa Owens

....

Wild West
An extract from a short story

After the dip of the second big hill, I took a turn onto a narrow road, following a sign that said 'To the Beach'. It was flanked by hedges for the first few yards, which gave way to a handful of bungalows – peculiarly English-looking in the rural west-of-Ireland setting, and they made me think of Eastbourne or Bournemouth, though I had visited neither. A couple had been recently spruced up: ugly windows with chunky white frames, walls painted the colour of margarine, bright dinky cars parked primly in the driveways. The others were careworn: missing tiles in the roofs, windowpanes opaque with dirt, plastic bags scattered in the overgrown gardens.

'Come and get your lemonade! Lovely lemonade!' A child's reedy singsong pitched through the quiet.

In front of the second-to-last bungalow was a fold-up table, manned by two little girls. A sign written in pink highlighter on lined foolscap was taped to the front of the table: 'DELISHIS LEMONADE!!! ~~50 cents~~ 20 cents!' The designer had run out of space – 'lemonade' was all squashed together, and the last three letters and the exclamation marks tumbled down the side.

'Hi,' I said.

'Hello,' said one of the girls in a small voice, suddenly bashful to have a customer. She was gap-toothed, seven I guessed, and her stringy blonde hair trailed down her back. A thin braid woven in grubby thread, alternating in sections of pink and green was growing out, fastened at the end with a bright green plastic bead. She wore a denim skirt and a cropped pink T-shirt that said 'Princess' in glittery writing and exposed the pale, gentle curve of her belly. She held herself with unthinking contentment, a child who had yet to be let down by her body. She eyed me breathing deeply, inflating and deflating her stomach like a balloon. Her business instinct kicked in after a beat.

'Would you like some of our delicious lemonade?'

'How much is it?' I asked. 'Twenty cents?'

'Yes. It used to be fifty, but no one was interested,' this was said matter-of-factly, but with a sorrowful shake of the head. I looked up and down the deserted road, and then up at the dull sky.

'Not ideal trading conditions,' I said.

The other girl was smaller, about three or four years old and her dark hair fell into her eyes. My mother would have described her as 'brown as a berry'. My grandmother, had she been alive, might have plumped for 'gypsy brown': a beautiful even sun-baked tone, a far cry from the all over pinch-sore redness that blighted my childhood summers. She wore a blue polka dot swimming costume and a ratty fleece hoody. Her arms were full of a cat explosion – a shock of grey fur with scornful yellow eyes. She sucked on the two middle fingers of one hand, squashing the creature in the crook of her elbow.

'What's his name?' I said.

'It's a she,' said the older girl, 'Katy Perry. So will you have some lemonade or what?'

I felt inside the pockets of my skirt, and my hands closed around a coin – a British pound. 'Hit me,' I said. 'I'll take a glass.'

'Twenty cents, please,' said the girl.

'I'm good for it,' I said.

'Show me the money!' the girl said, and I laughed.

'I'll give it to you after I've had my drink.' She sighed again and rolled her eyes, and from a plastic picnic box hauled a dusty two-litre bottle of TK Red Lemonade. A curling orange sticker on the side said €0.99.

'Wait,' I said, 'it's not homemade?'

'No,' said the girl, struggling to unscrew the cap. 'I didn't say it was homemade. I said it was delicious lemonade.'

'True,' I said. 'That's quite a profit you're making, even with the discount.' I tried to do a calculation in my head but gave in as the liquid hissed awake. The girl tipped the bottle slowly towards a plastic cup, and white foam cascaded out and all around it.

'Shhhugar,' said the girl. She righted the bottle and handed me the wet cup.

'Hey,' I said, 'there's hardly any in here. Look.' The foam had died away leaving a shallow red pool winking at the bottom. She let out a strangled noise, as if this really was the very last straw, and sloshed in a few more inches.

'Cheers,' I said, raising the cup in a toast. I knocked the lemonade back in one go and gasped. It was the stuff we used to drink at my grandparents' house – so sweet and fizzy it burned your mouth. 'Delicious indeed,' I said.

'Twenty cents please,' said the girl, extending her arm so her flattened palm was right under my nose.

'How much is this?' I pointed to a glass dolphin the size of my thumb. Half the table was colonised by cups, and on the other a selection of items were displayed on a striped tea towel. A miniature naked baby doll kept the dolphin company, along with a packet of shiny pink stickers and an ornate perfume bottle with a line of amber fluid at the bottom.

'That's mine,' the girl said. 'It's not for sale.'

I pointed to the doll. 'How much is that?' The younger girl twitched and mewled in distress, fingers still in her mouth, and the cat leapt away and trundled off down the road.

'That's Cara's,' said the older girl. 'She's called Baby Bethany.'

'It's too small to be a baby. Babies are about this size,' I put my hands shoulder width apart. 'Maybe it's been scaled down to size for a child using the adult-baby ratio. I guess most dolls aren't life-sized. Except for the scary life-sized ones.'

'What?' the older girl said. 'You're weird.' She made lazy circles with her finger at her head, and then pointed at me. 'You're a weirdo.'

'Just thinking out loud.'

The girl squinted at me, though the sun was deep in the clouds.

'How old are you?'

'Guess.' I said.

'Umm. Seventeen,' said the girl.

Cara pulled her fingers out of her mouth and wiped them on the hoody. 'A hundred!'

I shook my head. 'Thirty.'

'Woah,' said the older girl. 'That's old.'

I nodded. 'Guess what my job is.'

'A … teacher,' guessed the girl.

'A mummy!' Cara said.

I shook my head, pointed at them in turn. 'No and nope.'

'A – a shop lady?' said the older one. 'Give up.'

'Communications officer,' I said. The girls looked unimpressed. 'For the council,' I added. The older one sucked on the end of her braid. I picked up the perfume bottle.

'My sister and I used to sell perfume that we made from rose petals mashed up in water,' I said. 'You ever do that?' They shook their heads. 'I stole some roses from my neighbour's garden. I got in a lot of trouble.' I had spent a long evening howling in bed, nursing my smacked hands between my thighs. My sister had somehow escaped scot-free, and couldn't stop smirking while she tried to sympathise. 'It didn't really smell of anything.'

Behind the girls a door banged. A man appeared, straightening his shirt. He was about my age, maybe a bit younger, smallish and swarthy and handsome. I noticed the front-window curtains were closed.

'A customer!' he said, grinning at me, and Cara ran and jumped into his arms. I felt foolish and shy and put the perfume back on the table.

'Hello,' I said.

The man kissed Cara all over her face making loud smoochy noises.

'I'm off, miss. Be good for your mammy, what?' I blushed, thinking for a moment that he meant me.

He set the girl on the ground. 'Hey, Alana, give us a smile,' he said to the older child, and she obliged with a gummy flash. 'See ya now,' he said to me, and hopped into the white van parked on the drive. He reversed, revving loudly and disappeared down the narrow road.

'Was that your daddy?' I asked.

'Nooooo!' said Cara, giggling.

'That's Brian,' said Alana. 'He's our plumber. Daddy's in England for work. He comes home at the weekend.'

'And what does he do, your Daddy?'

'He's a plumber,' said Alana. There was a pause. 'Hey, you still owe us twenty cents.' Out shot the arm. 'Give.'

'Listen,' I said, 'I'm going to level with you. I don't have twenty cents.' Alana's mouth dropped open. 'You tricked me!' she shrieked.

'Wait! Wait, I have something better.' I took out the pound coin and placed it in her hand. 'It's from England. It's better than twenty cents, you can ask your dad next time he's back. It's like –' I still hadn't gotten to grips with the conversion rates, and took a stab in the dark, 'eight times as much? I've paid more for one tiny cup than the whole bottle cost you.'

Alana studied the coin and Cara stood close to see it too. Their heads were touching, bright blonde and dark brown. 'OK?' I asked.

'You shouldn't have lied,' said Alana.

'I didn't technically – but it's a great deal for you. In fact,' I picked up the doll, 'I should probably have something else as well.'

'No!' said Cara and snatched Baby Bethany from me. She jammed her fingers back in her mouth, tucking the doll under her arm and glowered through her fringe.

'I'm kidding!' I said, and crouched down to Cara's level. 'I'm sorry, I was joking.' She shrank away. Alana picked up the packet of stickers and examined them.

'I suppose you can have one of these,' she said. 'Not the butterfly or the cupcake. Or the bow.'

'Why don't you decide which one I can have?'

She stared at them, her fingers hovering above one then another.

'Close your eyes,' she said, and I did, wavering slightly on my haunches. My eyelids fluttered and I could feel her breath on my face as she came close, then a light pressure on my breastbone.

'Open.'

I looked down. A lonely pink heart shone on my chest. I straightened up.

'I should get going. The beach is this way, right?' I asked, pointing. The girls nodded. I held up my hand to Cara.

'High five?' She swung her free palm to mine, with none of the impact the build-up promised.

'Down low,' I said to Alana and moved my hand away when she brought hers down. 'Too slow.' She stuck out her tongue. 'Thanks for the lemonade. And the sticker.' I turned to leave, glancing at the window, and saw the flash of blonde hair and a bare arm disappear as the curtain fell back into place.

The beach was deserted. I stood at the tide line and watched as the sea crashed forwards and receded without a fight. The bay curved around to the left, and across the water a lighthouse stood right on the edge, facing out to America. I crunched back a few feet and lay on the chilly stones. A while later I felt something brush against my legs. Propping myself up on my elbows, I watched Katy Perry trot down the beach, her tail a smouldering plume, until I couldn't see her anymore.

A fat drop of water exploded by my hand. A few seconds later, another landed on my foot, a shocking icy kiss. In less than a minute the ponderous sploshes had evolved into out-and-out lashing. I pulled myself up and ran over the stones, back the way I had come.

On the bungalow road, the girls had abandoned their stall to the rain. I paused at the table. A couple of the plastic cups had tipped over and rolled to and fro, while the others were filling up. As water hit water, rich notes rang out – a musical riff against the general roar. Baby Bethany lay orphaned in the grass, her arms reaching out as though asking to be held. The red lemonade was still on the table. I seized it, shoved it under my jumper and dashed away through the thick wet curtain.

....

Lisa Owens is working on her first novel. She read English at Emmanuel College, Cambridge, and worked in publishing for six years – first as an assistant at an international literary agency, and then as an editor at an independent publishing house. She lives in London.

Julianne Pachico

Welcome

Welcome to my tree home. You can leave your walking stick propped there against the trunk. Go ahead and take off your flip-flops; it's easier to scramble up if your feet are bare. Watch out for those nails; if you're not careful they'll tear a hole in your clothes. You can sit here next to me, or if you're not scared, you can climb up to that Y-shaped branch. It's a bit high, I know, but you get a great view up there. You'll be able to see everything.

That building over there to the left? That's the landlord's garage. Celia got stung by a flying black insect when she was pushing her way through those bushes at the entrance. You'll meet Celia later. Anyway, for now it's nice just to sit and look at the leaves. I like those rowboat-shaped ones; when they drift down it's like they're sailing away on an ocean of air. Oh, of course, help yourself – most of the mangos should be ripe by now. But just so you know, mango skin burns your lips if you bite into it without peeling it first. If you want, you can always climb back down and eat the squishy overripe ones there in the dirt. It seems to be safe, for now.

I'll bet you're thinking that my tree home isn't that fancy, right? I haven't even made a nest to sleep in yet, like the ones you've probably seen woven out of palm fronds or plastic bags. But for me, this has been doing just fine.

Not everyone's so lucky to have a tree home. That old couple, what were their names: Willy and Maria. They were stuck climbing those rusty monkey bars. Lord, how they would shout on and on about how numb their legs got from sitting for hours on that sharp metal.

Then there was that young kid in the army boots, Roberto. He only ever climbed roofs: the house, the garage, the shed. Veronica, now she just walked straight through the garage door and climbed one of the rickety metal tables, the ones covered in bags of white powder, and lay down on top of them like they were fancy pillows propping her up.

You sure are lucky to be here with me right now, and not all by yourself.

I don't usually climb much higher than this, no. I'm glad you asked – the branches get pretty thin up there. I prefer not to take any chances. Besides, it's nice right here, isn't it? We have a great view of that pretty bush by the papaya tree, the one with the heavy white flowers. You can only see the river behind the fence if you stand, but listen closely and you'll hear the water tumbling over the rocks. The river should be clean by now – when Celia and I first got here, the water was filled with shredded white and manila folders that danced around crazily in the water. Laura was there too, sitting in the mud and thrusting her arms in and out of the water, over and over again like she couldn't stop herself. Celia asked her if she was looking for something she'd dropped, but she didn't answer, and when she pulled her hands out we saw that they were filled with streams of wet unwound black video tape, heavy and dripping.

If you think you can stand up on this branch without falling, you'll be able to see the brick wall with the shards of glass on top that surrounds the landlord's property. You'll see the water fountains, the Cupid and angel statues with their chipped wings, and the empty cages where he used to keep his animals: the peacocks and the monkeys, the lion and the rabbits. You look tall enough; you might even be able to see into the garage, see the bags of white powder resting in neat rows on the metal tables, the empty gasoline barrels and stacks of suitcases. Who knows, you might even be able to see the swimming pool. It's more of a concrete hole filled with leaves by now, but sometimes I close my eyes and think about what it must have been like once, the water so clean and blue it could hold a perfect reflection.

The landlord? Sure, you can ask about him. I'm not sure – he might have gotten a flight out of here to Europe or Australia, back before things got bad. Or maybe one of the paramilitary groups got him and now he's tucked away in the house somewhere, spread out on his big white bed with a machete sticking out of his chest.

Lonely? Why would you want to ask about that?

Well. I guess it was nice when I could see Willy and Maria over there, swinging their legs back and forth, and I could hear Willy shouting out their children's names while Maria just screamed nonsense. Whenever I felt like it, I could stand on this here branch and see Laura by the river with her arms in the water, and Veronica lying down in the garage, a red trickle of blood hanging from her nostril like a fancy jewel, and the sun glinting on Roberto's rifle, where he left it on the drainpipe.

Let me tell you something: sometimes I like to lean over this branch right here and picture Celia leaning against the trunk, where she first sat down with her hands pressing against her insect bite. She sat like that without moving for hours, you know, before she finally fell over sideways, and the blood that leaked out of the hole in her neck stayed in the dirt for days.

You sure do ask a lot of questions, don't you? You remind me of someone I used to know – I can't remember who just now.

Make sure you watch the sunset. I love how it looks when you tilt your head back and watch it through the leaves: slicing through the branches, bloodying the sky. The colors make me think of the grapefruits Celia and I used to pick on the farm back up on the mountain, by the village and the well. You can't ask about the well. The well is of no concern to you. But anyway, back then I still had my machete to dig up yucca roots. Boy, I would sweat getting them out the ground, but it was worth it. Those yucca roots are so heavy, you feel like you're carrying around the arms and legs you cut off someone's body. At sunset we'd walk through the underbrush to sit by the stream and listen to the hum of the insects as they shed their skins. The sunshine, the grapefruits, Celia's smile under her hat – let me tell you, that was all I needed to be happy.

That may have been the happiest I've ever been, actually.

You're being pretty smart right now, sticking so close. I mean, just think about the world for a minute and the state it's in. Really think about it. This world's gone to the dogs, and I don't mean the mangy packs that wander in here from time to time, poking their noses into the ashes of the abandoned barbecue pit and chewing on burnt pieces of wood. I mean that it's a real mess out there. Sometimes I tell myself that there's a meanness in this world that I have to get away from, nothing but meanness, but when I look at the bloody fingerprints on my pants that haven't faded, that's what tells me that it isn't something in the world, it's something in me.

The children will be here soon enough. They're the only ones who still come by here, you know. Everybody else left long ago: Willy and Maria with the ropes around their necks, Veronica with the jewel in her nostril, Laura with the stones in her shirt, Roberto – you know, I don't want to talk about Roberto.

It's getting darker now; the sun is almost gone. Mind yourself in front of the children; keep your voice down, you don't want to alarm them. Listen, here they come with their bedsheets and wooden carts and crusty nostril rims. Look how they settle down so nice and quietly, sitting cross-legged in the dirt, leaning against the barbecue pit. They're so good at tying the knots on their plastic bags to keep the ants and wasps out of their mangos. The way they're craning their necks back and turning their faces up – don't they make you feel like the tree is a fire and they're all sitting round it, just waiting for us to tell them a story?

You can't ask about the well. I said that already.

I don't know. The one thing I'll say about it is that maybe years later somebody will wander back up there – assuming that people are still left, of course, and we're not all skulls and bones lying inside of houses with machetes sticking out of our chests. Maybe they'll make it to the farm and find all my grapefruits, now huge and swollen and the size of coconuts, yucca and ferns growing beneath the house floorboards. If they can find the farm, they can find the red dirt road, and if they find the red dirt road they can find the well. Maybe they'll walk up to it and lean over, the crumbly brick pressing against their stomachs, and look deep down inside. I bet you anything they'll say that the bones belong to dogs, the smallest bones to rats. They'll tell each other that the ragged remains of clothing were dumped there, the heart-shaped earrings and boots with silver spurs accidentally lost.

It didn't happen, you see. They didn't push them in one at a time. We weren't there on the hillside, watching behind a tree. We hadn't decided to walk to the village that day. No, we stayed up there on the farm by the river with the humming insects. It never happened. We never left. We didn't see how they lined everyone up outside the church or hear them questioning everybody about the guns that weren't there and that nobody knew about. We didn't see the camouflage pants or red armbands, the white lace underpants with pink ribbons trampled in the dirt. We didn't see the baby and how they threw it in – that was the very first one they did, the baby. We didn't see the women and the pregnant and the old. I've never heard broken limbs getting crushed into mouths that are still open and screaming. I don't know what it's like to finally turn and run, smoke in our eyes and the burning village at our backs.

I'm sorry to disappoint you. You must have me confused me with someone else.

But don't worry, I haven't forgotten – I did say you would be meeting her. Of course I didn't just leave her slumped against the trunk. There's a bush of flowers she liked, the white ones by the papaya tree. I wiped the machete off after digging the hole, and when I was finished with Roberto I threw it over the fence into the river. Then I climbed up here.

That was the first time I climbed. I haven't been back down since.

The sun's gone now, but if you wait just a bit longer you'll see the moon starting to peek over the glass shards on the wall. Actually, it might still be light enough for us to see our reflections, burning in the house windows. Look over there, can you see? That's you. And there's me, waving back.

....

Julianne Pachico was born in England, grew up in Colombia and graduated from college in Portland, Oregon. She is working on a collection of linked short stories, and has been awarded a studentship for UEA's PhD programme in Creative and Critical Writing.

Lauren Rose

....

Mt Tabor

O ur housemate Adam picked up some acid the night before. He burst into our room at 2am to tell us his news.

'We have to do it tomorrow,' he said in the dark, breathless. 'It may be the last sunny day.'

Jack and I weren't sure, in the middle of the night, if he had actually come in and talked to us; but somehow in the morning, we both knew what was going to happen.

We were going to take it on Mt Tabor in the afternoon. Mt Tabor used to be a volcano. Or at least that's what people said.

Adam, Hannah, Toby, Jack and I all lived together in a big yellow clapboard house, a happy, falling-apart house. Jack and I had moved in a month before, after finding them on Craigslist. We biked over after breakfast, one after another, with full stomachs and greasy hands. It was a short ride with minimal traffic – Saturday afternoon.

We met Adam's friend Pete in a meadow on the mountain. He was already lying in the grass, spread out next to his bike, which he had built himself. He had long angular limbs like a Keith Haring drawing.

'Hey everyone,' he said, touching his scant beard.

We sat together in the grass, our bikes and backpacks flung around us, the sun hot like a warm blanket. Adam had already divided the tabs, delicately wrapped them in tiny pieces of foil, handing one to each person with the care of a teacher handing out snacks at recess. I unwrapped mine and dropped it on my tongue, careful not to touch the surface with my fingers. Jack had tried it once before and had warned me not to touch the paper, said it would come off on my skin. It tasted like nothing, like paper. I hadn't eaten paper since I was in kindergarten and would hide strips in my mouth until they became soggy.

We all smiled.

I reached into my backpack and pulled out my jug of water and my camera. I fell back in the grass and looked at the sky through the lens, at the shards of green grass like criss-crossing mohawks, at Jack's profile. I hadn't taken pictures in years, but Jack had discovered we could sneak into the local college darkroom and use it for free. He was trying to help me get back into it.

*

It was my dad who taught me – he had showed me how to develop and print, even built a darkroom in an unused closet in our old house for my tenth birthday. He let me use his equipment and try his different lenses and filters, the ones he used for work, the fancy expensive stuff he cleaned and organized at the kitchen table every Saturday. His beer bottle placed safely on the floor, to avoid a spill.

'Just housekeeping,' he would say, and my mother would make a face at him as she scrubbed the counters and washed the dishes and did the actual housekeeping, orbiting around him. It started off funny, like a joke – maybe she found him a little lazy, but she loved his passion, and at his peak, he was a busy freelancer, his photos appearing in magazines and newspaper features. He was always buying new flashes and light boxes and lenses, and the developer and fix weren't cheap, either. She had to take on an extra shift to make it all work.

Eventually, in the years leading up to when he left, she stopped making faces at all, because her face was always set in a sad kind of grimace, like she might cry or shout at any moment. He stopped trying to make jokes to her and would only talk to me if I came into the kitchen.

'Dot, come here and look at this, watch how I do this,' or 'Dot, could you just clean these for me please?' He showed me how to polish lenses, spraying a special cloth with cleaner, holding it over two fingers, rubbing the glass gently, in tiny circles. Distracted and like we were doing the most important business in the world, even after he had stopped getting much work and everyone else had converted to digital.

My mother would bang around the kitchen if I helped him, but never said anything – towards the end she started a grease fire out of spite. Even then they didn't talk, as the flames rose and crackled and the fire alarm sounded. She left the room quickly, satisfied, and he was already a little too drunk to react. He sat by his equipment, dazed. Arthur barked over and over, agitated by the noise. I wondered if she would have just let the house burn down, with all of us in it, if I hadn't done anything. But I called the fire department and they came within minutes. My father disappeared a couple weeks after that, but for some reason in my mind he left that day.

*

I was coming up. That's what they call it, 'coming up.' Everyone was talking quietly around me, laughing softly. I felt good, happy and buzzy, not scared. To my right, Toby was softly flicking a lighter, making a scratchy sound, watching the flame appear and disappear. 'Amazing,' he whispered. The metal top was shiny and reflected the sun. Adam and Hannah wandered into the bushes, holding hands. They bounced like cartoons, receding quickly into the blurred green horizon. I smelled the lighter fluid, and the grass, fresh and clean from rain the previous night, and my ineffective deodorant mixed with sweet-smelling sweat.

Jack held a dandelion inches from his face, examining the intricate seeds that burst out happily, like a firework pausing.

'This is the most beautiful thing ...' he said.

I laughed.

'No really, look at it,' he said, thrusting it in front of my face.

I examined it. We blew them at each other, our hair coated in white fuzz. There were so many dandelions and we all went around finding them, stooped over like hunchbacks to pick them. Sometimes when I blew them, I spit accidentally.

'It's kind of like seeing what we'll look like when we're old,' Toby said, 'when our hair is all white.'

Everyone laughed.

'I think we'll look really nice when we're old,' I said, and everyone agreed. I took pictures of Toby and Pete and Jack, so we could see them later and remember what we'd look like in the future.

Adam and Hannah came back with some acorns, and Adam juggled them while we lay around him in a circle and watched the pieces fly around above us. I took some pictures of him, adjusting the shutter speed so the acorns would make blurry arcs. The ground below us felt warm and wet and alive, like it was ticking. I realized it was my watch. Hannah made a daisy chain and put it on her head like a wreath, and I found her difficult to dislike even though she was prettier and seemed less confused about everything than I was. She made me one too, and I wore it around my neck like a crazy necklace.

Pete sat in the dirt, removed from the group, writing in a small black Moleskine, his eyes squinting behind his thick black glasses.

'You look like an author,' I said, taking his picture.

I'd only met him a few times before, but he laughed. He had a kind laugh.

'I used to want to be one,' he said. 'But now I just write for fun.' He had a nasally east coast accent, and reminded me of Holden Caulfield.

Jack went off with Toby.

'Just going to have a wander,' he said. 'We want to see some birds. There are starlings apparently.'

The sky tinged purple and if there were starlings around, they were going to come out then. We had to have been there for hours at that point.

Starlings sounded nice to me but I was enjoying the field.

Pete sneezed. I didn't have a tissue but I said bless you anyway. He smiled and went back to writing. I laid back into the grass, and then I sneezed too, wiping my nose on my hand. There must have been something floating around, all the pollen from the dandelions.

*

I inherited his nose, I thought, as I pressed its narrow bridge, trying to coax out another sneeze. His eyes, too – green, they ran in his family. In the years after he left, when I would be out with my darker-eyed, delicate-nosed mother, no one could ever make sense of us as a pair. Was she my older friend? Was I adopted? I got her smile, though – small straight teeth, and a freckle on my bottom lip that my classmates made fun of when I was little. It is an uncomplicated smile: neither of us can help but grin when we're happy. He was always better at concealing his feelings.

'Thank God you didn't get his teeth,' she would say, especially after he left. 'His parents had to take out a loan for his orthodontia.'

It felt strange to look so much like someone who was so gone. I hadn't seen him in 11 years; we hadn't heard from him at all, and he hadn't paid anything in the way of child support, as my mother often grumbled. He took all his camera equipment, except for the 35mm, a few lenses, and a weathered leather bag, which he left for me. A handwritten note saying that he was sorry, that he loved me, urging me to keep taking pictures. He'd be back sometime, he wrote.

Such a stupid lame excuse for a note but I saved it, tucked into the back of *Charlotte's Web*, which my mother unknowingly gave away when we moved to a smaller house. He didn't write her a note, but even as a 12 year old I knew not to tell her about mine. It wouldn't have done anyone any good. He left most of his clothes, his battered Volvo station wagon, the boat-like car in which I would later learn to drive. We thought he must have called for a taxi in the middle of the night, gone to the train station or airport and shot off as far away from us as he could get. He had cancelled all his credit cards so we couldn't track him that way. It must have taken a lot of planning to disappear so thoroughly, especially for a drunk. We put out a Missing Person report but nothing came of it. They don't do milk carton ads for adults; grown men generally leave because they mean to.

Sometimes when I would walk into galleries, I wondered if I would see his work hanging on the walls. I imagined him running around America, away from something and towards something, taking photographs, breaking into high school darkrooms across the sleepy bulk of the country to develop them. I hoped he left for something really profound – something worth it.

*

'Are you sad?' Adam asked, sitting down next to me. It was wearing off and I was feeling a little cold and prickly. The sun had nearly set, the light was in-between and our faces glowed blue and sparkly.

'No, I'm OK,' I said. 'Thanks, though.'

'I'm really glad you moved in, Dot. You and Jack.'

'Me too,' I said. 'Everyone is great. The house is great.'

Jack and Toby came back then, dripping and laughing. They didn't see any starlings, but they had found a pond and gone swimming. It was time to go. Everyone else cycled back, but I walked my bike down the dirt path through the darkening trees, down and off the mountain, back into the city with its lights and its people. I was sober enough to bike, but I craved the stillness that walking allowed, the slowness and the space to think.

....

Lauren was raised in Los Angeles. She graduated *cum laude* from Kenyon College in 2011 with a distinction in English literature, creative writing, and photography. She is working on her first novel, set in Portland, Oregon, about a woman who moves into a ramshackle co-op as she searches for her missing father. It explores themes of habitation, loss, and community.

Colette Sensier

The Inhabitants
Extract from a novel

T he doctor's face moved towards the wild child. When he got too close his eyes split away and duplicated themselves, a line of tight black circles. She sniffed, aware only vaguely that he was male and for some reason unable to do more about it than twitch. She smelt the garden around him, its huge blanket of things, and the changes that had happened in it since the mornings. She itched to know what they were, but Henriette's hand on her shoulder kept her in place.

He moved back and his face came into focus again. When he bent to her toes, she saw the powder on his hair and the brittle fading patch at the back of his head. His finger and thumb touched her ankle. She wanted to kick but for some reason moving her foot was impossible. In the frame of his white hands touching her foot, she saw Henriette's familiar black thonged sandals and big feet, the fourth toenail hanging loose.

Then the man's face was back again. He touched her thumb and the swollen pad of her hand, and handled her thick wrist. This was risky, so she hissed. The doctor frowned.

Reverend Whittaker stepped out of the shadow of the smiling white bougainvillea. 'We've given her a nip or two this morning, Doctor. Arrack. She should be – '

'Yes, yes.' Dr Merseul took his fingers from the child's wrist. 'But this deformity – what on earth ...?'

'Nothing on it!'

Mme Merseul took a few steps back, but not too many: a magnet with two repelling poles, fear and curiosity. She smelt of musty pollen and human sweat, in heat at this time of month. There was a very bright pearl button at her neck, shining enough to eclipse the whole world. La Sauvage unhooked her eyes to enjoy it, making it grow then shrink in the sunlight.

Rev Whittaker puffed on his pipe. The aromatic smoke billowed back out of his nose, dispersing the gnats which had gathered by the little party, circling the raw offal in Henriette's pocket. 'Henriette's been caring for her for three months now. Henriette, tell Dr Merseul, have you found any evidence which might indicate how she's come to be like this?'

It felt all wrong to have the maid and La Sauvage standing beside him in the garden, where he read the Sunday services. Though they spent most of their time there, he was never present at the same time; when not drugged, the child still threw a fit if any man came near her. He had to watch her from the house as she hopped after the maid on four legs like a rabbit, and as Henriette 'walked' her on two feet, kicking her back legs to make them move in a straight line. He'd watched her gulping offal left over from his own meat – watched her lapping from a bucket of water like a little pet cat. But he'd never seen her up so close, not since she'd been let out of the net.

Dr Merseul said, 'What are her injuries, girl?'

'She favour she right foot,' said Henriette. 'And the big left toe, it bend over wrong. Like this.' She crooked her index finger. 'Like Lune finger. Lune finger broken since long time.'

Dr Merseul mused, 'A broken toe ... that might have prompted her to seek help here.'

Whittaker knew Lune: Courbier told stories about that family, how Billy Carpenter had bought his wife from a woman famous for her cruelty. He'd collided with her before in the village square, and noticed the scar running the length of her face. Hadn't her old mistress thrashed her servants with jellyfish tentacles?

'Why are you talking about Lune's finger, Henriette?'

'That how I know a broke bone, suh.'

Dr Merseul was kneeling, oblivious, palpating La Sauvage's foot.

'Yes, there's a break. But there's nothing to be done for toes. Perhaps she'll always be slightly lame. You won't get much work out of her.'

Whittaker coughed smoke. 'My interest is more scientific, Doctor. Have you heard of Wild Peter, for example, captured in the forests of Hamburg some years ago, who they say was suckled by wolves?'

The girl was flexing, trying to rise, her shift moving up and exposing her thighs. Mme Merseul took a step back and Henriette pressed down on La Sauvage's shoulder.

Whittaker continued, 'He lives at court now, I believe; the British court, that is. A favourite of Queen Caroline. Or there's the Fraumark Bear-Girl, kept in an asylum in Hungary for the last three years, and still eating only raw meat and tree bark. These were children cast outside society and abandoned to the wilderness, who've grown to be – something not quite animal, yet unmistakably far from human ...'

'But not spirits, surely, Monsieur!' Mme Merseul's hand fluttered to her throat, the pink muslin sealed with the pearl button.

'No, no, Madame. Of course not. But something deserving of investigation ...'

The doctor's hands still rested on the girl's left foot. 'There's certainly severe deformity. Caused – I'm not sure. She clearly exerts great pressure on the thumbs, the pads of the hands, and the flats of the feet. No arches at all. Peculiar.'

'I believe she uses them to leap between trees.'

'That might explain it. There's a sore on her leg as well – your maid can treat that with rubbing alcohol.'

'Henriette, can you get close enough to treat her now? We can't give her arrack every day.'

Henriette glowered. 'She let me touch she now. You saw, she got that gown on.'

Dr Merseul straightened up. 'My recommendation would be a course of bleeding. Bring her down to me, say twice a week – or I can come up to St Songy if you'd prefer it, Reverend, a few extra francs, that's all – and I'll let out some of the old bad blood. That'll have new human blood pumping in her veins in no time; and then she'll stop wanting the raw meat, and she'll get some liveliness back into her. It's very elementary natural philosophy.'

'Of course. Of course. God intended us to cook our food.'

'Well, there's no goodness in uncooked meat. And heaven knows, if an African slave can't digest regular meat, a ... a wolf-girl will no doubt have an even coarser constitution.'

It was no good. La Sauvage's fuzzy feeling was wearing off and the men's voices hurt her ears. The shining pearl button swelled, the one good thing in the garden, until she leapt to Mme Merseul and made a grab for it with her teeth.

'Oswald!'

Mme Merseul tumbled to the grass like a shot deer. The doctor batted the girl away with the flats of his hands, Whittaker apologised and apologised and called to Amelia to bring a glass of brandy.

Henriette grabbed the wild child by the back of the neck and pulled her away, past the red flush of rhododendrons and the Indian roses, back to her shed.

Rev Whittaker began to shepherd his guests up to the house, babbling, 'Please do dine with me, Madame, Docteur. A little nourishment will do you a world of good, Madame ...' The doctor cursed his wife for coming along. 'Don't talk to me about a "soothing female presence," Caroline – you wanted to see the gossip up close!'

'I'll have Louette prepare some tamarind juice, Mme Merseul; it has a very cooling effect ...'

Dr Merseul turned to the minister, looking angry. 'The speed of those limbs, Whittaker! No scoliotic patient should move as quick as that.'

'What did I tell you, Doctor? An uncommon phenomenon, surely ... uncommon.'

'I'm sure she's a ghost. I'm sure she's a demon,' sobbed Mme Merseul – a new wife she was, barely twenty.

The ocean was always audible, wherever you were in the village, a low roar echoing through the bamboo trees. But as they got closer to La Sauvage's shed – Whittaker had to pass it to take the Merseuls in through the front door – he heard something else, a roar in a different timbre.

'Is that her?' He could feel the doctor's wife shaking beside him.

'She doesn't like men. I'm not sure how much arrack Henriette gave her.'

The roar broke into syllables, loud thrusts of protest: shrieks like a baby's, then shrieks like a woman in labour. The shed's planks shuddered. And behind all that, Whittaker could hear a rhythm, the overlarge feet thumping the floor. Reflexively he touched the small sword in his waistcoat – only an ornament but effective enough, probably.

A gasp sharp as a pinpoint: Mme Merseul. Whittaker followed her eyes and he saw it.

La Sauvage was dancing a jig on the roof. Stamping and kicking her heels up high, as if there was no such thing as gravity, the pull of man towards the earth. She whooped, indistinguishable sounds which sounded inhuman, like monkeys calling to each other.

'That's no child, Whittaker!'

Whittaker saw it – the brown shift had slipped down and hung around La Sauvage's waist, showing two apple-shaped breasts which bounced at the crest of each jump. Mme Merseul picked up her skirts and ran towards the palisades marking the end of Whittaker's land. Merseul followed her.

Suddenly Henriette was standing beside the minister, her body in his shadow. Both of them, both the real people, stood frozen for a second, before the demon dancing on the locked, reinforced shed. Behind her a spreading flame tree bristled, a bright red background to the animal who punched the air now, her fist flashing metal against the scarlet light. A little knife in her palm.

'Where did she get the knife, Henriette?!'

'That not my knife! I don't let she in the kitchen!'

'Then how on earth – ?'

Henriette stepped closer to the shed and he followed her. She pointed at a little hole between the roof and the wall – a hole about the size of a kitten.

'No no – a rat couldn't fit through that. Someone must have left the door unlocked!'

Henriette turned her head – she was taller than him, and their eyes were level. 'We was watching, sir. You don't think we gonna see she open that door?'

The flame tree's red leaves rustled, ripples circling the girl as she launched herself into it. She leapt from branch to branch, and then into the white branches of oleander marking the Valois grounds.

'Henriette!'

The maid ran, not as daintily as Mme Merseul, through the stiff grass. Rev Whittaker stayed back as she cantered past the rose hedges, the orange trees, the bronze samovar, getting smaller and smaller as she went.

He wasn't quite used yet to the island's social mores. Grown women walked around hardly clothed on the plantations, he knew. He suspected it would be acceptable to pursue La Sauvage, half-dressed, around the village — to take hold of her on her bare skin, and restrain her against his body. But to act this way wasn't in his nature. He did not quite want to do it. So he stayed back, and went to the edge of the garden where olive-wood palisades marked his house off from the village, and watched Henriette career alone across the square, looking as if she too was running away.

Colette Sensier graduated from Cambridge in 2010. She's won young poets' competitions and been featured in anthologies, with a debut collection due in 2014. She's working on a novel — developed on a Spread the Word mentoring scheme — about a feral child in eighteenth-century Mauritius and its present-day ghost.

Julia Stuart

Chestnut Sunday
The opening chapter of a novel

Chapter One

Hampton Court Palace
May, 1898

On the day that Princess Alexandrina would learn that there were no words to describe accurately the stench of a week-old dead body, she stood at her bedroom window studying the antics in the maze. It was the same scene she'd witnessed numerous times over the last three weeks as she waited with increasing frustration for a response. There was William Sheepshanks, the keeper, sitting in his high chair overlooking the leafy labyrinth, his sodden Piccadilly weepers hanging down his cheeks following yet another downpour. He should get those whiskers trimmed, she thought. They didn't do him any favours. He was shouting directions to a tourist who, judging by his gesticulations, seemed to have been lost for hours. She peered at the visitor now scratching the back of his head. Yet another man who didn't know his left from his right. Not only that, but the fashion for waistcoats this season was double-breasted and buttoned high. Who on earth was his tailor?

The princess, nicknamed Mink on account of her childhood habit of sleeping amongst her mother's furs, looked up at the clouds, smears of sooty fingerprints across a forlorn sky. Was this really what her life had come to? Spain and America were finally at war, the House of Commons was debating the Evidence in Criminal Cases Bill, and yet here she was, spending her days staring out of the window criticising excursionists' vests. She'd been to Girton, for God's sake.

Three weeks. It had been three whole weeks since her advertisement for her new venture appeared in *The Times*. 'H H Princess Alexandrina, Private Detective. All enquiries Hampton Court Palace,' it read. Yet, she still hadn't received a single reply. Surely someone needed assistance, a lady perhaps, who wanted to keep things discreet?

She picked up her silver cigarette case, a present from her father, and studied the engraving of her grandmother hunting tigers on the back of an elephant. She lit a cigarette, inhaled, then blew the smoke hard against the window. So no one wanted her. She'd just have to find another way out of her financial mess. God forbid she'd ever resort to what some ladies did when their money ran out. She'd rather end up in the Kingston Union Workhouse down the road than become some greasy gentleman's mistress.

The door opened and Pooki strode in holding a silver salver. The princess was used to her ignoring servants' rules. The maid had looked after her since her mother died, when she was only six, and had the annoying habit of voicing her opinion, rather like a bossy older sister. But she should always knock on a bedroom door. Mink was just about to remind her, but the look on Pooki's face stopped her. She glanced at the tray and saw the reason for her excitement: a letter. God, had someone finally replied?

Mink grabbed the ivory opener, read the letter, then dropped it into the dressing table drawer.

Pooki frowned. 'Another bill, ma'am?'

It was, but Mink wasn't going to tell her that. She'd only get another lecture. She returned to her contemplation of the visitors outside, wondering why she hadn't had one response. Perhaps it was the same reason why no one invited her to balls or dinner parties anymore. As the daughter of an English beauty and an exuberant exiled maharaja, for years her oriental glamour had captivated women columnists. Happily for Mink, they also extolled her talent with a gun and quoted her calls for suffrage. Such was her position in society, every lady worth knowing longed for an invitation to one of her Highland shooting parties. But since her father had died in flagrante delicto with a maid – who spared not the slightest vulgar detail at the inquest in that God-awful accent of hers – she could quite understand why so many now viewed her as tainted.

Mink turned back from the window. She wasn't the only one to be shunned, she thought, glancing at Pooki. Most of the other servants at the palace refused to talk to the maid on account of her dark, Indian skin.

She stubbed out her cigarette. 'I'm going for a walk in the Privy Garden before it starts to rain again.' She waited for Pooki to fetch her walking costume.

The maid didn't move. 'You still haven't opened the pile of letters downstairs, ma'am. I can recognise your creditors' handwriting. Not that one though,' she said, nodding at the drawer. 'That's a new one. You must have bought something expensive. And I'm not talking about that pair of grey gloves I've just found. They look very costly.'

Mink put a hand on her hip. 'There's nothing more expensive than a cheap pair of gloves. The button-holes burst and the sides split within a week.'

'The cost of bread has gone up, ma'am.'

'And? The war's doubled the price of wheat.'

'Then you shouldn't have bought the gloves, ma'am. Nor the other item, which I'll find soon enough. You're just like your father when it comes to money. Don't forget what the palace housekeeper said – some residents have to leave because they can't afford to live here.'

Mink didn't need reminding. They'd only been living at Hampton Court for two months, and already she was worrying about expenses. A year after her father's death, when a place finally became vacant, Queen Victoria gave her a grace-and-favour home in the palace grounds. It was the least she could do, Mink thought, given that she'd exiled her father to Britain as a teenager after annexing his state of Prindur. He lost his sumptuous palace, the lucrative mines, and many of the family jewels, the best of which the Queen (or Mrs Fagin as Mink preferred to call her) kept for herself.

Despite the British giving him an annual stipend, he built up debts at the gambling tables, as well as at the draper's, the gunsmith's, the wine merchant's, the furrier's, the bootmaker's, and the exotic animal dealer's. When he begged the Government for more money, it gave him a loan, the price of which had been the house – their home – upon his death. Not that he mentioned the atrocious state of his affairs to Mink. It had taken a fatal heart attack and a subsequent visit from his lawyer to find all that out.

Pooki raised her chin. 'There may not be any rent to pay, ma'am, but you're still responsible for the heating, lighting, water and maintenance of the house. Speaking of which, the damp needs seeing to.'

'I'm well aware of all that,' Mink snapped. While most of the other residents, many of them widowed aristocrats who had also fallen on hard times, were lodged in apartments, she'd been allocated Wilderness House, the only thing available. The six-bedroom home overlooking the maze was proving unexpectedly expensive to live in.

'I'm not the only one in financial difficulties, you know. There's even less money around than last year. All those people lured into speculating are now suffering the consequences. The paper said even the South African millionaires aren't entertaining. Not that they'd invite me, of course.'

Pooki took a step forward. 'I wonder why no one's replied to your advertisement, ma'am. You should be busier than Sherlock Holmes, considering you solved the Major General's murder.'

Mink had assumed so too. She started investigating the Major General's death when Pooki became the main murder suspect. However, when she discovered who the culprit was, along with their motive, she convinced the police that the poisoning had been entirely accidental. The perpetrator had suffered enough at the hands of the Major General, she decided, and didn't deserve the death penalty. Her conscience was quite clear in that regard. But without a villain to hang, perhaps her detective work had made less of an impression than she'd thought.

'It's been three weeks, ma'am. You need another plan.'

Mink shot her a look. 'Have you come in just to put me in a bad mood?'

'No, ma'am, I haven't. Otherwise, I'd also have mentioned the fact that Dr Henderson hasn't called for a week, and you're in love with him, even though the whole of Middlesex knows he can't dance.'

Mink flung open the wardrobe doors. 'I'll wear my pastel blue walking costume and cream blouse. Would you get them down for me?'

Pooki remained where she was. 'That doctor has no money. And you're twenty-nine.'

The princess grabbed the clothes, and threw them onto the bed. She then presented her back to Pooki, her hands on her hips as she waited.

'I'm not in love with Dr Henderson,' she said when the maid finally started unbuttoning her scarlet gown for her. 'And anyway, no woman should marry for money. It'll end up costing her eventually.'

'I agree, ma'am. But that doctor needs to buck up his ideas if he hopes to marry the daughter of the Maharaja of Prindur.'

Mink wondered again why he hadn't called. It had been a week.

'Do you want to marry him, ma'am?' asked Pooki, fastening Mink's skirt.

'I can manage now, thank you.' The princess reached for her blouse. 'You may leave.'

The servant didn't move. 'You haven't answered my question, ma'am.'

Mink raised her eyebrows. 'Doesn't the library need turning out?'

'No, ma'am,' said Pooki walking to the door, her head high. 'I did it while you were staring out of that window thinking about the mess you're in.'

*

Mink buttoned up her broadtail and ermine coat, then sat in front of the mirror to arrange her toque. It was the one with the blue feathers she'd seen in a milliner's window in New Bond Street and managed to hide for several days before Pooki spotted it. She was careful not to flatten her hair, which she always wore in a padded chignon to gain a few extra inches. While she'd inherited her mother's blue eyes, unfortunately she had her father's lack of height. She fiddled with the feathers. There was always a chance that she'd bump into Dr Henderson on his rounds at the palace. Not that the man was a picture of elegance himself in that frock-coat of his. You wouldn't exactly mistake him for the Duke of York.

She wondered again why he hadn't called, and leant towards the mirror. She wasn't getting stout was she? All the worry about her finances was making her eat more than usual, particularly those Charbonnel et Walker chocolates. The last thing she wanted was to look like her father. His love of shirt-sleeve pudding had become the subject of music hall songs after he died and collapsed on top of that naked maid, trapping her with his bulk until she was rescued by the owner of the opium den. Or so the papers gleefully reported. God forbid that she'd have to go on the Banting diet or surrender to Madame Maigre's Corpulence Pills.

She was choosing a hatpin when the door burst open again.

'Ma'am! There's someone here to see you,' Pooki exclaimed from the doorway.

Mink turned round, her heart tight. 'Who?'

'Two gentlemen, ma'am. They wouldn't give their names.'

'Did they say what it was about?'

'No, ma'am. They said the matter was confidential. They must have seen your advertisement.'

She stood up, and threw her hat onto the bed. 'You'd better help me put that dress back on. I can hardly receive them in a walking costume.'

*

As she entered the drawing room, the two visitors rose from the settee like startled crows. One was the tallest man she'd ever seen. While he was reasonably attired in a black frock-coat, she noticed the broken brim of his top hat on the settee. His face was undefined on account of his surfeit of chins. He'd grown a pair of tatty whiskers, perhaps as camouflage or a distraction, which only inflamed the spectacle. As for his vastly shorter companion, he was wearing a brown suit, which was so ill-fitting it looked like he'd bought it from one of those sales of items left in railway carriages. He was smiling, revealing teeth that reminded her of a costermonger's donkey. But worst of all was the whiff of smoked herring. This pair weren't *Times* readers, she thought. They couldn't possibly have seen her advertisement. Who on earth were they? And what were they doing in her drawing room?

· ·

Julia's first novel, *The Matchmaker of Périgord*, was longlisted for Spread the Word: Books to Talk About 2008. Her second, *The Tower, the Zoo, and the Tortoise* (2010), was a *New York Times* bestseller. *The Pigeon Pie Mystery*, published in 2012, was selected as an Oprah.com 'Book of the Week.'

Michelle T Tan

Arrivals

T he man was still staring at her when Gwen turned to look. He sat on the bench to her left, leaning back against the hole-punched steel, arms folded, head tilted towards her. She flicked him an irritated glance and returned her attention to the flat screen. PR 467 from Seoul, 11:30, status: delayed. Gwen uncrossed her legs and tapped her right foot impatiently. It was only 11:07. She had been sitting in the arrivals lounge for almost half an hour already, and she had a headache.

It was one of those mornings. She had woken up late, with a hangover, and had had to skip breakfast and a shower to rush off to work. Chris, her boss at the Ateneo's Office of International Relations, had looked at her like he was about to have a seizure. She'd been working there less than six months, and already she'd accumulated an embarrassing record of late time-ins. It was only by a few minutes, never more than fifteen, but the habit irked Chris no end. She never called in sick, and she worked hard, but it was her chronic tardiness that reflected most on her performance.

'Don't,' Chris said when she started to explain. 'Just go.'

At first Gwen thought she had been fired, then she remembered that she was supposed to fetch a group of Koreans from the airport today. She grabbed a folder from her desk and ran out to find the driver. She spotted him in the parking lot, leaning against the university van, coolly enjoying a cigarette.

'Let's go, Manong!' she said, climbing into the front seat. 'Go go go!'

It was only later, as they were weaving in and out of traffic along Aurora Boulevard, that Gwen realised that she had been panicking for no reason. According to her folder the plane was scheduled to land just before noon, which meant there was still a good three hours to go before the meet-up. She threw the folder on the dashboard and let out a laugh that quickly developed into a groan. Manong looked at her suspiciously. Her head was beginning to throb again.

Even with the heavy traffic in Pasay, they arrived at NAIA Terminal 2 with more than forty minutes to spare. Manong dropped her off at Arrivals and told her to call him when she was ready to leave. Gwen bounced out of the van and entered the terminal.

Now it was 11:07 and she was in a sourer mood. The seats were cold and uncomfortable. A stranger was ogling her. The flight was delayed. She was getting hungry again. Earlier she had bought overpriced coffee and a sandwich from a nearby café, but now her stomach was grumbling anew. Gwen continued to stare at the blue screen, idly hoping for another update. She ran her tongue over a small bump on her lower gums, courtesy of this morning's hasty brushing. She was sure it would develop into a nasty sore.

It wouldn't be so bad if she was here for family, or a friend at least, but instead she was waiting for a bunch of exchange students. Gwen never liked exchange students. She didn't mind corresponding with them through email, but meeting them physically was a different matter. Six months wasn't a long time to judge, but she'd had her experiences. It wasn't anything they did exactly – which made it hard to explain to friends who cared to listen – but rather their overwhelming sense of entitlement. As soon as they arrived, the students took on the usual foreigner's airs, and the politeness of previous emails would give way to condescension.

Normally Gwen didn't mind so much. It was part of the job, and, anyway, they were usually gone in a few months. There were even some nice ones who brought her gifts and sent grateful emails after they returned to their own countries. But today she was nursing a hangover, and she couldn't help but project her gloom onto the Koreans, as if they could somehow be blamed for her present misery.

She never should have gone out with Trish and Pam last night. They had spent several hours at a bar in Timog, downing cheap cocktails and complaining about their boyfriends. Trish and Pam both worried about marriage. They dropped hints to their men and fretted about being too forward, kept silent and grieved about turning into old maids. It seemed a peculiar anguish. They were at that age when they could still be single but were no longer young; the dreaded almost-thirty.

Gwen listened disinterestedly. She was only a few months younger, but she didn't yet share the same concerns. Marco brought up the subject sometimes, but they never talked about it seriously. Neither of them was in any hurry. She had just quit her job at an attorney's office and was now trying out working for a university. Being on campus gave her a feeling of youthfulness she had almost forgotten. On evenings like the previous one, she felt wild and irresponsible. She felt twenty-three.

From somewhere overhead Gwen heard the two-note tinkle signalling an airport announcement. A woman's voice: 'Flight PR 467 from Seoul has been delayed and is now scheduled to arrive at 12:10 pm.' She checked her watch and uttered a quiet curse. In front of her, passengers from another flight were already making their way along the wide concourse, clutching passports and dragging suitcases behind them. Along the metal railings stood family members, lovers, travel agents, taxi drivers – the latter two holding up signs bearing mostly foreign surnames. A few shouts and questions, and a moment later they were exchanging hugs and handshakes, smiles and claps on the back. Gwen stared at them dully. She had seen this same performance only fifteen minutes ago.

The crowd dispersed, and the flow of passengers dwindled to a trickle, lone stragglers walking leisurely towards the exit. Suddenly there was a small commotion – a man had rushed past the others to reach a woman on the other side of the railings. He dropped his bags. There was a long embrace, a longer kiss. The other passengers filed past without taking much notice.

Gwen had been texting Manong when she looked up and noticed

the couple's reunion. Her hands relaxed their grip on the cell phone. The scene, common enough in an airport, jolted loose a bundle of feelings in her. She experienced a strange conflation between life and memory, when what was remembered became real, ushered in by that most mundane sight, one of those unexpected convergences that matter little in the span of a life, but mean so much in the moment.

Almost six years ago she had stood in this same airport with Niko. He had just finished his OJT at the Peninsula Manila, where she worked as a receptionist at the time, and was going off to be a cook in Qatar. His family was based in Cebu, so he had planned to go to the airport alone, but she had insisted on accompanying him at the last minute. That taxi ride from Tondo to Pasay was the longest she had ever taken. It was a distance of only fifteen kilometres, but inside the vehicle time seemed to slow and thicken, toiling in the insufficient air conditioning, almost coagulating between them.

She and Niko said goodbye at the Departures drop-off. He was running late, so they only had time for a curt hug and some hurried words before he had to go. Years later, Gwen would forget exactly what they had said, if they had promised each other anything. But even now she could still recall the sight of him approaching those doors, showing his papers to the guard, and turning around one last time to wave before disappearing inside the terminal. She remembered his jacket, a bright blue Adidas knock-off, getting smaller and smaller as he walked away.

Sometimes Gwen wondered what had become of Niko, but never enough to try to find him. The last time she talked to their friends at the hotel, they said they hadn't heard from him either. But that was a long time ago. Now she sat thinking about him and those months they shared together many years before. She wondered how long he had stayed in Qatar, if he had since returned to Cebu, or if he was even now in Manila, perhaps living only a few streets away from her but nonetheless a stranger. She wondered if he had managed to open his own restaurant, which he had always talked about doing. She thought about herself back then, the weeks she had spent crying over him, and marvelled at how far life had taken her.

Gwen considered all these things with a kind of nostalgia. But sitting there on that cold steel bench, she felt no sadness, only an awareness of the years spanning that existence and now. She looked down at her cell phone and finished composing the text to Manong. She checked her watch. There was still so much time left to kill.

Michelle T Tan hails from Manila. She has been published in *Philippines Graphic and Philippines Free Press*. Her story *Her Afternoon Lives* won second place in the 2012 Nick Joaquin Literary Awards. She is working on a collection of short stories about the lives of ordinary people in Manila.

Sara Taylor

Things You Can't Forget

2007 –

Miscarry. See a doctor. See a shrink. See your mom's priest and decide that you fundamentally oppose marriage. Sign a twenty-year mortgage with Seth and refuse to answer when your mother asks if you are sleeping together.

Dream about Jake sometimes and be surprised that these dreams don't terrify you. Wake up considering the possibility of meeting up again, finding out that he's a decent person. Think that maybe you've forgiven him; you've forgiven all of them. Panic when you see someone that looks like him in the produce section of the grocery store. Read the obits and the police notes on Sundays with a hopeful eye: the fuckers have to die eventually.

2006 –

Wonder where Jake lives now, if he tells whomever he's fucking about his crazy bitch of an ex that is you. Wonder where Richard lives now and get that sick feeling. Don't think about Donnie. Bring extra work home so you don't have to get into bed, close your eyes, try to fall asleep and fall into night terrors instead. Wear Seth out because sex is the only thing you can do without thinking. Argue about kids; decide to wait a few more years. It's a moot point all ready. Join the eight percent of women who get pregnant on oral contraceptives.

Keep living. Flinch when men get too close. Hear breathing in your ear, thick and wet, when you're sitting at your desk or walking at sunrise or any time at all. Seth tells you that you shudder in your sleep sometimes, but you don't cry any more. Panic comes out of you unexpectedly now, like a demon possession, like hose water through your fingers when the pressure's too high. Control it around your mom, who still asks, 'You sleep on the couch when you visit Seth, right?' in the way that's the answer, not the question. You give the right answer.

2003 –

Have your first orgasm with someone other than yourself, and wonder when you got serious about Seth. Get a real job doing paperwork in a law firm. Go out for margaritas with Laura when you go home and laugh your ass off at her imitation of the message Jake left on her phone: 'You LIED to me! I can't believe you did that, I was so good for her!' Ask each other how it took him a whole year to figure that out. Wish that you could keep her with you.

2002 –

Meet boys who think they understand you, sleep with them for your own reasons, break it off when they start getting too serious or too rough. Graduate and go home for a visit – your parents want you to move back. Call up Laura to go out, but she asks you to come see her first because there's something that she has to tell you. She starts with, 'I understand if you don't ever want to talk to me again after this, but I can't keep it a secret from you any more,' which makes you wonder if she's going to say that she's in love with you, but what she says is, 'I got Jake to dump you. I told him you were sleeping with other guys and doing crack and planning on dropping him anyway, and I'm sorry that it hurt but I'm not sorry that I did it.' Then she starts crying and you start crying and you're both crying on each other but it's the best you've felt in a long time.

Meet a guy named Seth, who isn't freaked because you cry in your sleep, and slowly stop screwing other people.

2001 –

Jake still calls you, sends you emails, wants to 'catch up' (sometimes), and at other times demands that you apologize because 'you know what you did, don't pretend that you don't.' He says that if you keep ignoring him he'll tell your parents, and for once you call his bluff. You tell your dad that he's acting crazy, won't leave you alone. Your dad calls him, talks to him once – you don't want to know what they said, don't want to know if Jake outed you – and the calls and messages stop. The nightmares don't.

Start talking to your mom, but carefully. She doesn't know the questions to ask. You wouldn't be able to answer if she did ask.

Take a road trip with Laura over the summer. Fuck everything that moves. Worry about finding a job when you graduate, but not too much. Have moments that you can't predict when, even though you're standing in the pasta aisle or riding your bike or sitting in class, you're really pressed against a cinderblock wall, feeling a hand pulling you up by the hair, moist breath on your skin, your self-ness clawing its way out of your body as you try to hold it together.

Wonder what you did wrong, or if you're just unlucky.

2000 –

You can't sleep in your own room, you're scared to close your eyes, so you bring your books over to your friend Richard's, flop on his bed while he sits at the computer, do your work while he does his and catnap to the sound of his typing. He knows about Donnie, and he has a girlfriend, back home, that he wants to marry. You think you're safe until you wake up on your back with all of your clothes off. He's on top of you and his breath in your ear is thick and wet and slimy, and you try to push him off, say you don't want to. Afterwards he says that it never happened, that no one can know, and you walk back to your dorm with semen running down your leg.

Go home for the summer. Your mom talks to you the same way she talks to your fourteen-year-old sister, which is like you're both eight. You roll your eyes at each other.

Laura says it wasn't your fault, what happened. You don't believe her.

Work a lot and read a lot and try not to throw up when you get messages from Jake. Seeing his name in print makes you nervous; you hope that you'll never see him in person again. You answer your phone one day in September and his voice on the other end says, 'Happy birthday, bitch,' and your throat closes up and you can't move. Afterwards you try to laugh because he got the date wrong, but you can't.

1999 –

Self-medicate with scotch and weed, just enough to get through the nights. Don't go home for the summer. This pisses Jake off; he tries to make you move in with him and you're glad that you can't, even though you want to. He screams at you. When he's really pissed off he describes the other girls he's sleeping with, how fantastic they are in bed. Laura wants to know what's wrong, and you don't tell her all of it, but you tell her that you want out, you want out but you're scared of what he'll do if you tell him that you've had enough. Then you borrow a car and drive eight hours to see him. He leaves you locked on the front step in the rain for half an hour. You blow his mind, but when you get back the refrain has changed from 'you suck in bed' to 'you suck for never having done that before.'

School starts again. See Donnie around, have nightmares while awake, self-medicate more. Decide to go pre-law, wonder why you're so miserable. Get a call from Jake at midnight the Sunday before midterms: it's over. You're over. He can't believe that you'd lie to him like that, that you'd use him like that. The line goes dead without you saying anything, and all you can think is, what the fuck is he talking about? The world ends, for you, a few weeks ahead of schedule.

Start sleeping around to make the Jake-hurt feel better. He starts calling again, wants to stay friends, but still isn't going to forgive you for 'what you did.' Every time you ask him to spell it out for you, he gets angry that you're playing innocent and hangs up.

1998 –

You've forgotten how to talk to your mother.

Jake has sex with another girl while you watch. This makes you sick every time you think about it. He tells you to get used to it – he'll stay with you while you're at school but you can't expect him to say no to other girls.

He comes to see you the night before you leave, comes in the back door around one am, kisses you, then puts his hands down your pants. You don't want to, not with your parents asleep upstairs. He says that if you don't be good he'll wake everyone up and tell them what kind of girl you really are. You do what he wants. It's not the first time.

Start college, not at the place you wanted to go but the place you can afford. You tell your parents that you're staying at school for fall break, borrow a car, and go see Jake. In the parking lot before you leave he takes your toll money; you try to get it back and he grabs you by your hair, and suddenly cops are pulling you apart. You tell them it's nothing, he's never hurt you, you were joking, and they let you both go. You get back to school an hour before your first class, go to take a shower and see just how bruised you are under your shirt. You are relieved that it was dark and the police couldn't see.

Go to a party, drink too much, make out with a guy named Donnie. Wind up in a bedroom with him (still making out), try to leave when he takes your shirt off, but he's stronger than you are. Ask yourself afterwards why you didn't scream, why you didn't fight harder. Jake cries when you tell him, and then sleeps with another girl. Stay drunk for a week, sober up to take antibiotics for the infection Donnie gave you and find yourself screaming on your bedroom floor.

Your aunt sees you kissing Jake. When you come home your mother is crying: how could you do this to her, she raised you better. She asks, 'Oh my God, you two aren't having sex, are you?' in the way that's the answer, not the question. You give the right answer. Your grandmother asks, 'Che cosa?' over and over, and your dad tells you to explain to Nonna why your mother is crying.

They tell you to break up with him, so now you have to stick it out.

Laura asks about the bruises on your arms. You tell her that they're from the gym.

1996 –

You and your best friend, Laura, skip Saturday Mass to go get ice cream; a guy named Jake stops to talk. He wants to get with Laura, but Laura isn't interested so he starts talking to you. You start meeting up on the regular. At some point, the kissing goes farther than you're comfortable, but you don't say anything because you want him to like you. He tells you that no one will want a virgin, that you should lose it when you have the chance, and one day without planning to or meaning to it happens. You think about confessing to the priest, but worry that he will tell your mother because you're only sixteen. Decide that it won't technically be a sin, if you stick it out and get married, if he's the only man you ever sleep with. Hope that you aren't going to hell.

....

Sara Taylor is from Virginia, which has produced a taste for moonshine and occasional unintended forays into the Southern Gothic mode. UEA has been a part of her overly complicated plan to explore beyond the borders of the US. She is currently working on two very different novels.

Sharlene Teo

Goodbye Armadillo

The Internet is down forever. We tried troubleshooting but it's an irresolvable issue, and everyone is afflicted. You can't fully be angry at something when it is happening to everyone. Loose-leaf impersonal anger just feels shitty and unsatisfying. It's like hitting a brick wall with baby mittens.

Without the Internet my brother and I sit bored at home, gawking at desktop wallpaper. It is just the two of us in a four-bedroom flat. We can scarcely afford to keep the other two rooms empty, but we can't bear to dress them in strangers. Our parents succumbed to cardiac arrest in quick succession seven years ago. Our youngest brother decided that the only way to cope was to move to the other side of the world. He was always a quitter, always a snail. I miss him ridiculously. Up until last week he was only contactable by email.

My older brother and I have no friends besides each other. We aren't disagreeable. We didn't mean to discard everybody else; it just happened. We filled our evenings with the Internet and now we don't quite know what to do with all this ticking time. The array of alternatives makes us tense and uncomfortable. We jump at the hiss of a kettle. We agree that it is too humid to stay outside. We are too grown-up and unco-ordinated for ball games, too young and illogical for Sudoku. The television flickers on. I switch it off. I lack the hope and patience for prime-time television serials. I feel like I can't relate to all these fish-ball sellers' daughters with their marmoset eyes, their hearts of gold.

I lie on the food-stained sofa and imagine the Internet as a dead animal. Flopped out in front of me, an ancient armadillo – corpulent, perverse and wrinkled. I picture its greyish-pink, dirty neck rings and sad, beady eyes. I've always thought 'sad' was a lazy way to describe eyes, but this armadillo would have such sad eyes. Just a huge, leathery armadillo excavated from the earth and strung up like a birthday banner. Where would they put it? Probably in the National Heritage Museum, where it would set off all the smoke alarms, and scare passing children.

I'm trying to read a book. After I lost my job a few months back, I decided to try hard-copy concentration, a habit so casually and inexorably neglected over the last few years. Now that the Internet is gone I will have to work even harder to finish reading a whole novel. I've picked a book called *Tangled Thoughts of Leaving*; medium-thickness, yellowed, with an extremely ugly forest of purple vines on the cover. Wilfully hideous, those dark messy vines – crude and almost pubic. That cover is what caught my attention when I found it in a second-hand bookstore. It is by an author I have never heard of, some Danish guy with an unpronounceable name.

The story is about a mild-mannered, middle-aged man whose wife runs away to the jungle, leaving a note citing 'irreconcilable differences'. He tracks her down in a cannibal estate, blunders through mosquito-ridden canopy, and almost starves to death before discovering and getting into a fight with the chief cannibal. Through the revival of his long-forgotten judo skills, the husband manages to overpower the chief. The chief, cowering, asks the husband to spare his life, and he obliges. Just as the hero turns away, the chief sticks a hunting knife in his back. 'Too bad! It's a dog-eat-dog world,' the chief says. The husband lies doomed and sputtering blood on the floor. 'Just tell me my wife is OK,' he pleads. 'Tell me she's having hot showers and proper meals.' The chief sniggers disdainfully and turns away. The chapter ends.

I'm only at the halfway mark and cannot imagine things progressing much further. I dislike the wife and didn't think much of the husband. I don't believe or buy into any of it and I am wondering if I am one of only about ten people to have ever tried to read this lousy novel. I try describing what has happened so far to my brother.

He thinks it is all about mid-life crises. He says it is so clichéd, done to death and fake-o, the whole mid-life crisis thing, never mind the mangled marriage. I tell him you'll never really know until you get there, will you, and he shrugs.

My brother is 35, and I am 27. Depending on what direction his health goes, maybe he's already middle-aged. When we were younger, when he was younger, he was incredibly handsome. He looked not even a bean-root related to our younger brother or me. He had strong, sharp features framed by commanding eyebrows, the kind of fresh-milk face to mould onto a coin or affix to a keychain. Even I had to admit his handsomeness, in my awkward phase when it felt tongue-bitingly icky to do so. I don't know what happened to him once he hit 30 – a churning-through, smudging-out process. He sort of puffed up, filled out; his features got a little erased. Now he has an indistinct, bleary face, which elicits no questions. Back then he was something special.

At school, at tuition class, on a crowded train, all these random girls would put love notes in his backpack when he wasn't looking. Folded and re-folded squares of paper tenderly frayed. He never admitted to reading them, but he would announce he had received some rubbish as he came through the door, and throw the notes in the bin on the way to his room. As a child I used to take the letters up from the waste bin and pretend I was a handsome boy, reading a declaration from Amanda or Min Li, any fawning one. For a moment, scanning my eyes over pastel-coloured ballpoint scrawling, I could almost believe I was eighteen, and a dashing boy, and that I couldn't care less. I kept all the love letters in one of the cardboard boxes under my bed.

I was skim-reading *Tangled Thoughts of Leaving* two days ago when a scrap of paper fell out of the last few pages. I picked it up and unfolded it.

'Dear you,' read the note – smudged-blue Red Leaf pen scrawl, handwriting half-familiar. 'I don't know if you've seen me, but I'm the girl at the bus stop at 7:15. I'm the one who is always looking over your shoulder at what you are listening to on your MP3 player. I'm that girl. My name is Tracy. I have short hair and a polka-dotted uniform. And I love you, yes, I love you, sweetness.'

'I found one of your notes,' I told my brother when he returned from work. He works in a subletting office with four other people, and now that the Internet has died everything takes a long time more. They sit around piles of yellowing fax paper, frowning and miscalculating.

'Throw it away,' he replied, and went to heat some soup up on the stove. That's another thing – all the microwaves stopped working a few months ago. Every microwave on earth played a polyphonic goodbye and shut down forever with one shrill, final beep. I'm ready! exclaimed the microwave. I'm ready to stop waiting all the time, I'm going to go now.

'Don't you want to know what it said?' I protested. I never let my brother know that I usually read all those notes. He probably knew anyway, but didn't care. When I thought about it, my older brother was such an impervious person. He didn't even cry at our parents' funerals. The last time I saw him display alarm or much noticeable emotion was when he fell down and broke a leg over twenty years ago, and even then, he had only squawked and looked mildly irritated. Unlike my younger brother with his penchant for sappy music and slow-stewing sulks, my older brother is habitually blithe, clement-tempered, that droopy ex-handsome face betraying not even the slightest trace of disappointment. His main interest and hobby up until recently was an online multiplayer game called WARtal. So much for WARtal. His entire arsenal, award badges and P2P chat logs gone up in smoke.

'Aren't you a little curious?' I asked, still holding the note.

'Not really.'

'What if it's new?'

'Nah. No idea how it turned up, but definitely not new. Bin it.'

And that was that. I thought of Tracy, this frozen sixteen year old in a butterfly and Blu-tack room, uttering her prayers and tucking that scrap of paper under her pillow. Sleeping On It. I pictured a nondescript, plaintive face, daydreaming in moonlight. And that note had found its way, years later – to me, to us. I felt sorry for her. And I also felt spurned.

My brother settled on the sofa with his bowl of lemongrass soup. He stirred the soup, and murmured about the news.

'What else do you think will go next? Magnets? Television?'

'I don't know.'

'When will you find a new job? I can't support you forever.'

'I know.'

'You know, you shouldn't –'

'Shouldn't what?' I asked. There was brittleness in my voice. I pushed it out through my teeth, like a tiny fish bone. I sounded old.

'Never mind. I forgot what I was going to say.'

The spoon clinked against the side of his bowl.

I frowned and scrunched the note in my palm, and then I went outside for a cigarette. I thought of all the cigarettes I had ever smoked or wanted to smoke lined up in a row. Some just tiny little stumps and others straight-backed and flawless, paper tar soldiers snaking all the way down the road.

In the air I heard chanting. It sounded like they were holding a memorial service in the nearby community centre. They were always holding memorial services in that green, broad linoleum-floored venue but the chanting today sounded louder and even more mournful than usual.

Five white cars floated past. Propped up in their back seats I thought I saw wreaths and framed photos of a tired and rusty armadillo. If I squinted I could even picture it in better detail: that scaly, honk-nosed, dustbowl face. Such fine features, for an armadillo. I missed the Internet. My heart gave a little.

Scientists had said that magnets were losing their attractive force. They were groping around for a solution – working around the clock, organising emergency conferences. It was quietly terrible and extremely important, because magnets were in so many things. Without a magnet, what would hold a fridge together? It would just be a lidless cupboard of food.

The sky was brownish-pink and smelled of incense. My body slackened, ready for sleep. There would be a few more soft, small hours to go before bed. Maybe I would finish that book, or maybe not. I unfolded and read the note for perhaps the twelfth time since discovery, careful not to get ash on it. I inhaled my cigarette and thought about what I used to do before I got fired. I used to take the 7:20 bus to the park near my workplace. I used to sit in the park, the one with the empty Speaker's Corner and the reflexology path in the shape of a snail. I would take my breakfast there, black coffee and half a soggy bun, and look at the birds. And I used to think aren't you always going to be here. You and me in the morning, little birds.

· ·

Sharlene Teo studied law at Warwick University before working in publishing. Her writing has appeared in places such as *Esquire* and Q*uarterly Literary Review Singapore*. She is the recipient of the 2012/13 Booker Scholarship and the 2013/14 David TK Wong Fellowship.

Goodbye Armadillo

Suzanne Ushie

Moving

An excerpt from a short story

The driveway was narrow. Bluish paint peels hung limply from the walls, all the way up the tapered staircase, down to the small landing where a gaping sun window let in warm gusts of Lagos air. Inside, Khinde gasped: an alcove and newly-laid tiles — rarities in an old duplex in Mende. The apartment was more expensive than all the others she had seen. But after six months of checking adverts in Castles, six months of endless phone calls and crushing house viewings, she wasn't going to lose it. She got out her cheque book, already imagining a serene colour scheme. But Baba Femi laughed and said the landlady wanted to meet her first. He inhaled in a way that made her anxious because she had heard stories about nosey property owners.

'Does she live here?' she asked.

'Nooo. How can?' Baba Femi chuckled. 'Madam doesn't come here sef. She lives in Ikeja GRA.'

Khinde regarded his lean face, his high cheekbones so incongruous for a man, and wondered whether or not to believe him. Her colleague in the publishing firm had recommended him, assured her that he was different from all the other estate agents, those who said a house was 'under renovation' when its foundation was being laid and 'finished according to your taste' when it had a bathroom with no shower and sink. Baba Femi had given her no reason to distrust him so far — at least all the houses he had shown her had roofs — but there was a lurch of nerves in her hands, even after he said, 'Don't worry sister. Madam will like you.'

When Khinde met Madam, a sixtyish-year-old woman with grey hair that stuck out from under a stiff ochre headwrap, she felt as though she should be still in the presence of this tiny woman who would command respect in a room full of tall people. But Madam was warm, a little too warm, while Baba Femi did the introductions on the terrace in her vine-enshrouded house. It was unusually hot for January. Khinde's hair clung to the back of her moist neck; yet she didn't touch the glass of iced tea a maid placed before her. There was a steady churn of apprehension inside her. She looked down at the manicured garden, fascinated by the three-tier fountain shooting elegant arcs of water. She strained to follow the conversation which was mostly in swift Yoruba. At some point Madam asked Baba Femi about his family. Khinde shifted on the wicker lounge and wished they would go straight to the matter.

Finally, Madam turned to her. 'So what do you do for a living?'

In different circumstances Khinde would have laughed at Madam's newly elevated accent, neither British nor American but certainly non-Nigerian. She kept her face straight. 'I'm an editor. I work in Mimmoret Books.'

'I see,' Madam said, leaning forward in her chair. Khinde could tell from her flat tone that she hadn't heard of them.

'And where are you from?' Madam asked.

'Cross River.' Khinde expected the question. The owner of a cosy flat in Ikeja, a middle-aged man with a bump-covered chin, had taken one look at her light complexion and said he didn't want an Omo Igbo who would choke his house with a battalion of relatives, an unmarried girl at that who would no doubt also have a clutch of lovers. Khinde said, 'But I'm not Igbo,' and the man laughed and laughed as if he had heard that a thousand times.

Now, Madam said, 'Interesting place. I taught in a secondary school in Calabar years ago. You people are nice but very laidback.'

'No we aren't,' Khinde blurted.

Silence fell. Madam's expression was unreadable. Baba Femi started to speak Yoruba, keen to maintain the peace, to cool flared-up egos so he would still get his 10 percent commission.

Khinde knew she would not get the apartment. She had, after all, played the enraged defender. She had raised her voice. The dream of moving out of her aunty's flat was broken. Then Baba Femi turned to her and said, with a sly smile, that she was free to move in whenever she liked.

*

Khinde wandered around her sparsely furnished apartment, a frosted glass of Star in hand. She placed it on the sill in the balcony and glanced at the faded red kiosk across the street. The world had taken on a surreal sheen. She now had a place of her own. She would no longer mute her Miles Davis CD when her aunty walked in so she wouldn't be asked, in the usual whispery voice, why she was listening to 'old people's music.' She could wear her permed hair without being told that weaves were invented for a good reason, that she would scare men off with her resolute plainness. It worried her aunty most. And when Khinde said she was moving out, she had glimpsed that fright on her aunty's contoured face, in her wounded speech. An unmarried young woman, her own niece, living alone in Lagos? No way. It was troubling enough that Khinde didn't have a proper job in a bank or a telecoms company and now this? That day, it took almost two hours of playful persuasion – along with a bottle of J'adore – to receive her aunty's blessing. Her aunty, in turn, gave her a farewell gift: a set of non-stick pans she knew she would never use.

Now, she smiled as she walked into her bedroom and lay on the mattress whose lumpy filling reminded her that she needed a bed frame, a microwave, a charcoal painting or two. It was nauseating, the scent of fresh paint, but her choice of mint green for the walls and crisp white for the trim made it more bearable. She heard scattered cheering from outside; probably the men in the neighbourhood barber shop, electrified by a Premiership match on TV. Her eyes were closed for about a minute when a knock sounded at the front door. She didn't get up. She suspected it was Tega, the lean-muscled young man who lived downstairs. He had offered her a lift in his sleek Honda and asked her out to dinner right after she moved in. She couldn't decide why he amused her. Perhaps it was because of his cloying sense of entitlement, or his grave nod whenever she turned him down, as though in a matter of time she would come to her senses and realise she was his. She heard the knock again, three weak taps, and then silence.

On Monday, when she returned from work, the gateman welcomed her with a hushed, 'Madam dey inside o.' A ladder was leaning against the house. A shirtless man stood on it, sweating, chipping off flecks of wood from the roof decking. Madam sat under a shade, her headwrap awash with polka dots. She called out orders. You missed that spot. Don't hit too hard. Be careful, this property is very expensive.

Khinde said, 'Good evening, Ma.'

Madam glanced at her then back at the shirtless man. 'Seyi, she is back.'

It was troubling, the evenness of Madam's tone. Khinde's temples began to throb. 'What is the problem, Ma?' she asked.

'Seyi, did I say there was a problem?'

Seyi replied with the jocular eagerness of a servant agreeing with his master. 'God forbid bad thing, Madam.'

Madam turned to Khinde. 'What I meant, my dear, is that we were hoping you would come home in time to clear out the mess on your balcony. As you can see, we have a lot of work to do. In fact I sent Seyi here on Saturday to inform all the tenants. He knocked on your door but you didn't answer.' She smiled in a way that made Khinde feel underdressed.

'Sorry, Ma. I'll clear it now,' Khinde said.

Later, as she dumped the empty beer crates – the previous occupant's 'mess' – in the yard, the smallness of her own voice began to annoy her. Surely Seyi could have left a message with the gateman. Besides she had paid her rent. She could keep a bloody horse on her balcony.

Back in her apartment she switched on her laptop to watch a movie. It was difficult to focus with the steady clink of the hammer outside, with the unyielding momentum of Madam's voice. She was there again the next day and the day after; supervising the digging of a gutter, acknowledging greetings from passers-by, giving more ridiculous orders. Whenever the noise was unbearable, Khinde wildly imagined that Madam would demand to makeover her apartment. Until she got home one evening and found the renovation complete, and Madam gone.

Late one night, the power went off while Khinde proofread a manuscript. In the yard she found her I-Better-Pass-My-Neighbour generator outside the shed, its long grey cable unplugged from the socket. She pointed the torchlight to the left and saw that her neighbours' generators were unplugged too.

The gateman mumbled, 'Sorry, sorry,' even before she finished complaining. Every tenant now had to keep their belongings upstairs. Madam's orders. The shed was going to be demolished.

Khinde knew, then, that she could not handle a screeching machine right outside her room. She phoned Baba Femi and embellished the story so he would sense the urgency of it.

'Baba Femi, are you still there?' she asked. He had been so quiet that she thought he had hung up.

'Yes sister.' He cleared his throat. 'Look, Madam is not a bad person. She just likes to do things her own way. You know she is a big woman. But I'll talk to her. She should allow you people keep your generators downstairs.'

'And why did you lie to me? You said that she never comes here.'

'Calm down. I'll call you tomorrow.'

He didn't call. What he did, instead, was 'flash' her. He ended the call immediately after the first ring so she would call him back. She was downloading music in her office. When her mobile phone vibrated she went into the restroom.

'Baba Femi, what did she say?'

'Madam did not agree o. She even told me categorically that she will return your rent money if you like.'

Khinde stared at the air freshener on the wall, and thought of pouring the greenish-gold fluid into the sink, emptying her rage. She was irritated by his stark ineptitude, by his smug inflection when he said 'categorically', as though he merely wanted to show off his knowledge of the word.

'Give me her number. I'll talk to her myself.'

'Ah! Nooo! I don't want Madam's trouble abeg. Let me talk to her again, you hear?'

The call end beep sounded. Baba Femi would not persuade Madam any further because he knew, he had always known, the kind of person she was. What piqued Khinde most was not the awareness that she had been conned, but the fact that she had been conned by a partial illiterate.

....

Suzanne Ushie studied English and Literature at the University of Calabar, Nigeria. Her work has appeared in *Saraba*, *Sentinel Nigeria*, *Overtime*, *Fiction Fix* and elsewhere. She lives in Lagos and looks forward to a time when she will no longer write advertising copy.

David Whelan

··

Bad Cooking

SUGGESTED MENU

Cullen Skink

Lemon Sorbet

Filet Mignon, Asparagus Frittatas

Rasogolla, Sandesh, Coconut Barfi

A Bottle of Château Lafitte

After removing the head, I melted the flesh down in the bathtub until it resembled a particularly lumpy porridge with that swirl of raspberry jam I so detest and, then, to equal out the acid, I added three cups of sodium bicarbonate and four litres of milk before seasoning with thirty tablespoons of vanilla, six cups of Chinese Five-Spice, one kilogram of caster sugar, fifteen whole eggs and, though the recipe did not call for it, a thimble of my own tears.

Love, in any animal, brings out the greatest depth of flavour in the meat.

After spending a brief moment admiring the beauty of the severed head (such curious blue eyes!), I blended the mixture and moved it to the freezer.

Ice cream must always be left for at least an hour to set, though I could hardly wait. As my father used to say:

'The quickest way to a man's heart is through his stomach.'

*

I suppose that I first dreamt of becoming a chef the moment I successfully sucked upon my mother's balloon-shaped pink nipples.

This is what psychologists call the inciting incident.

My childhood evenings in our home in Sussex were spent in a heated sweat of voyeurism – I was impossibly shy and, due to a stammer inherited from my father, was much more comfortable writing than speaking. So, I contented myself scripting wild recipes into my diary from the windowsill of my second floor bedroom, which commanded an impressive view of the two hundred acre grounds, and secretly salivated over the plumpness of my mother's chickens in their coop beneath the sycamore or, when they were sold off, sufficed myself on the brief sight of my neighbour's gangly limbs and blink-and-you'll-miss-it bottom.

Other times, when there was no one to watch but my own mulish reflection, the grass resembled upturned bones and I retreated to my bed, and read Freud, Nietzsche, Thomas Harris, Samuel Pegge.

*

By age twelve, I was convinced that my awful older brother had inserted a cockroach inside my favourite stuffed bear (name: Captain Snuggles) and that one night it would dig its way out of the thing's belly and crawl inside my mouth as I slept. As my fear became too much to handle (I could tell you of being kept up at night by the scratching of the tiny legs inside the stuffing), I decided to decapitate the Captain to find out what was inside once and for all.

I had fantasies of cooking the bug for my brother on his return from school under the guise of a lamb tagine.

Apparently, my mother discovered me asleep by the pond, covered in white cotton dried into red blood.

In my desire to find the truth, I had sliced open the skin on the underside of my index finger and, due to an aversion to human blood that I have only just scaled, passed out beneath the stars, sucking on the wound.

*

My mother convinced me of my homosexuality the summer she caught me changing into her Cleopatra dress.

'You should join the local tennis club,' she said, as she did up the straps. 'Lots of lovely people there.'

'By people do you mean boys?' I asked.

'Well, we don't want you playing with girls, now do we?'

*

(Sitting here now, a doughy one-time-three-starred-Michelin-chef in soiled evening wear, I wonder if my desires were ever truly motivated by sex or anything similarly animalistic. I am still as God made me.)

*

Picasso said his greatest inspiration was his cat.

I am, sadly, allergic.

*

When I was old enough, and had proved my sturdiness by surviving five years at Eton (a period that began immediately after the bear beheading incident and which included, among other juvenilia, the forced ingestion of another student's severed hallux after a particularly heated game of fives), I moved to London and took a sous position at The Ivy, which taught me everything I needed to know about bad cooking.

After I had garnered sufficient respect and means (my parents' death by a fire that consumed our entire house; my eldest brother mysteriously killed a week later in a hit-and-run), I moved to France.

Well, to the Frenchest part of London.

I was never any good at foreign languages.

My restaurant, named Tarrare after the legendary Parisian appertísta (consider the word born, Oxford), gave me great joy and inspiration for the majority of my life.

Throughout the nineties and the fledgling years of the new millennium, hardly a day passed by when my taste buds were not tantalised by the sweet waft of haute cuisine emanating from the huge open plan kitchen; there was a constant stream of coq au vin, ratatouille, ragù, and croquettes of all varieties …

But artists become bored.

It is in their nature.

I, for instance, became bored at around the same time Lehman Brothers declared bankruptcy.

A year passed before my restaurant went under.

If it weren't for my beloved Matthew, who worked as a lawyer in the adjoining office, I would have been on the streets.

*

Boredom leads to one of two things:

1) The bottom of the bottle (pref. a cask of Château Lafitte, mais bien sûr).

2) Experimentation.

Or, in my case, both.

Three years prior to all this I had picked up a small book on the life of a German gourmand and technician Armin Meiwes.

His advancements in the ideas of recipe (a true chef, he maintained, must always love his ingredients) and variety (a story about the transformation of pork into ice cream enticed me for weeks!) had lingered in the dark corners of my mind like vermin under the floorboards for some time, and it was only after I had spent two years rotting in anonymity that they began to resurface.

*

But poor old Armin!

There is a misconception about people of his ilk that comes from what I call the Hannibal-Carib Binary Problem.

Simply told: in the minds of the masses, they are either uncivilised brutes feasting on the gluteals of their enemy whilst their wives hollow out various humerus bones into well-fitting and fashionable cod pieces or impossibly well adjusted and successful snobs with penchants for nice Chiantis who just so happen to enjoy the intriguing and deep textures of Americana sautéed.

This is simply not the case.

As human beings, they are bound to the same base laws of nature as ourselves. They burp, snot, shit and – gasp – even fall in love!

Armin's meal was, of course, someone he loved deeply.

*

The more I thought on Armin's words, the clearer my life became.

I started to see myself in him; I started to see myself in all of them.

Sociopathic vs Tribal. Lecter vs Chief Mawindu.

What absolute rubbish. Pfffffft. (Reading Instructions: Mouth open half a centimetre, lips puckered, teeth together, blowing softly as if you were sending a kiss to a lover spied sipping a macchiato on the corner of Old Compton Street only to realise, mid-blow, that he is accompanied by a daintily dressed and completely non-doughy 'Unknown', which reconfirms your admittedly paranoid suspicions, and, then, in an attempt to mutate the kiss into something resembling a noise of disgust, raise the tongue to the roof of the mouth, press so hard you think that the muscle may rip in two, and tut. As loudly as you damn well can.)

Some of them, believe it or not, are just as fucked up as you.

*

(Did you know that you can buy an eighteenth-century guillotine from Sotheby's for only five hundred pounds? And that, after slipping a tenner to the movers, you can have it installed in its fully functioning capacity in your living room for your francophile lover to come home to and praise you for your sense of compassion, devotion, taste?)

*

My point being, after the economic crisis ground my restaurant between its taut buttocks into nothingness, I became increasingly dissatisfied by the influx of peasant food in the capital.

After one proto-fast-food restaurant flooded London, the rest appeared overnight and drowned all of the truly worthy restaurants in a watery Béchamel sauce.

Far be it from me to assume your walking habits but what insatiable student of flavour has not rambled down Wardour Street or across Rathbone Place and been affronted by such abortable chimeras as burger and lobster, rice and apple, bibimbap cupcake, or soup and hotpot?

We were trapped in a culinary nightmare dictated by tawdry trend above purity, experimentation, love, with no escape in sight.

Love!

Of course, by then, I was also in love.

That ever-distracting, heart-fluttering, intelligence-destroying disease. Anyone who says they have produced great art whilst in the midst of some delectable orgy of passion is either a liar or in grave need of a visit to the Louvre.

Yes, you see, the aforesaid mentioned lover was none other than my dearest, sweetest Matthew, who saved me and then, foolishly, betrayed me.

Move over, ladies.

Hell has no fury like a gourmand scorned.

*

I suppose my jealousy was birthed unto me from my mother, who spent her few days away from her filmset gluing her ear to the door of my father's office or picking up the second house phone whenever she suspected him of deviousness.

Eventually, when the string of phantom lovers grew too long, she was sent away to Broadmoor.

But I digress.

*

I first suspected that Matthew was promiscuous after we had been together but a month. Originally, I was fine with it: I didn't care for sex, and I was happy to see him receive physical satisfaction from others as long as they remained entremets between the main courses of our relationship.

But after a time, things changed.

He systematically broke plans, made reconciliatory ones and then broke them again. I was confined to the kitchen, and ordered to cook him bouillabaisse, rouille, crepe flambé, which would all go uneaten.

Oh, how these things tortured me about my former glory!

Later, over drinks, I would catch the whiff of ramen clinging to his jacket, or spot the yellow circles of burger grease on his cuffs as he reached for another glass of wine.

I even attempted seduction, but he fell asleep some time between our discussion of Ming vases and the lighting of incense.

So, I did what my mother taught me to do, and followed him.

I found him with his head between the legs of an Iranian transvestite in the downstairs toilet of one of those terrible de rigueur fast-fooderies.

To tell the truth, I was more appalled by the betrayal of his palate than my heart.

He had propped the door open with a half-eaten box of potato wedges.

'Matthew,' I said.

'Mmm,' he said, though perhaps not to me.

I knocked gently with one fist.

'Gfha?' A noise akin to popping a lollipop out of a mouth. I glimpsed the slim pink frills of ladies' underwear around a hairy ankle.

'It's me.'

'Ah.'

I nudged the door open with my foot.

'So this is what you choose to eat?'

*

I dragged Matthew back to the house.

I plied him with drink, we got savagely pissed, he maintained his innocence (caught red-handed!) and eventually I smashed him over the head with a bottle of my precious Château Lafitte.

He went down like a sunken soufflé.

I pulled the guillotine out from its place beside the fireplace, certain now why I had bought it.

The head rolled around the floor, eyes burning like twin sapphires.

I poured myself a glass of wine.

*

(Alcohol, as a general rule, assists most things.)

*

Have you never – like a symbiotic parasite – been bound to another soul so deeply that, in your madness, the only way you can think to preserve them is to consume them?

Have you never felt a pull inside your chest so strong that you think your entire body may, at any moment, implode?

Have you never been to Paris?

David Whelan, 24, is from London. He is Reviews Editor of *Litro Magazine* and Short Fiction Editor of Fleeting Books. He has been published in *The Guardian*, *3:AM Magazine*, Shortfire Press, *nth position*, *Gutter* and *Untitled Books*, amongst others. He's working on a novel about an unsolvable mystery.

Matt Zandstra

Private View

F riday evening and the city squirmed after work. Suited men
and straight-skirted women hubbubed at the corner doors of
pubs. Restaurants buzzed and sizzled, waiters all young and really
something else, and everyone on their way, coming and going. Beer
and wine and water all fizzed, and Coke went the way of all Coke.

The pub had that jaunty nautical thing going on. Brass instruments
and ships' wheels. Booths and partitions. It looked to Harry as if half
the company were here. He thought at first she was one of the art
department crowd.

She said, 'And what do you do?'

He waved his hand, 'Brand stuff,' he said.

'You brand stuff?'

'I find the stuff of brands.'

'That sounds like bollocks.'

'What about you?'

She was tall and she was named Vanessa. Dark hair, chestnut
maybe, feathered at the fringes. She had very long fingers which she
held extended as she spoke. Her mouth was wide, and it quirked at
the corners making everything in the world seem a little slanted.

'Oh me,' she said.

Office workers broke onto the bar. It was like a war, like the
beaches, wave after wave of them, and he and Vanessa in this still
place, with her fingers, strangely stiff and her mouth quirked.

'And really. What do you do?'

'Art stuff.'

'The stuff of art?'

'I can show you.'

*

The word WORK was projected onto the building in a big bold font. An 80s FRANKIE SAY font. Harry looked up at it.

'That's you?'

Vanessa stood beside him, very close, and he felt something faintly electric from her. It was summer and their bare forearms brushed. He was a little drunk.

'That's me.'

The building was a slab of Regency, porticoed and iced white, its lower windows were hidden beneath poster boards which showed images from previous exhibitions. There was a neat holder for brochures screwed to the wall beside a large, firmly shut door.

A name was projected just below WORK.

'Vanessa Michaels,' he read. 'So is that work as in your work?'

'It's work as in the world of ...' she said.

There was an alleyway at the side of the building. Metal wheelie bins, the smell of piss, and a stubborn drift of last autumn's leaves. The passage opened out into a mean concrete yard. There were two moulded plastic chairs, and an ashtray between them. There was a door, featureless and cheap, a metal panel around the lock area to make it harder to break in. She pulled a wriggle of keys from her bag.

'I know Marco,' she said, as if that might mean something.

Harry crowded her accidentally as she opened and entered. He didn't touch her, but his body cupped the crook of hers slightly. He had a flash of them fucking in a gallery. That room in the National with the Hogarths – all those syphilitic whores and rakes looking down on them doing it over the cushioned benches at the room's centre. And, oddly, a bored attendant watching too. No photography.

They walked through offices, a few mismatched desks, old carpets. Little crusts of personality clustered under old-fashioned monitors. A mug with pens in it, a photo of a child grinning beside a summertime boat. A plastic daisy chain. Harry kept his own desk entirely clean. Leaving such signs behind seemed to him a dangerous practice.

And then on out into the gallery proper. It had the illicit, caught-unawares feel of public places in their private moments.

'Take a look.'

She disappeared into a side room, and he heard the sound of a fridge opening. Glass tinked. A cork squeaked. Fluid gurgled.

Harry stood in the gallery's central atrium. He could feel the air move in it. Above him were paned skylights, and the floor was a varnished beach, a light sandy colour. Merciless white walls.

*

The paintings were actually photographs, he thought at first, filtered in a way that brought up their primary colours and made light fluid, everything more beautiful than it should be. But then, he thought, they couldn't be photographs at all, at least not undoctored photographs. There was a confusing motion in them. They moved constantly but remained entirely still.

A young man stood, solicitous, in a shiny suit beside a barred door. He held keys and a brochure. A teacher pointed to a whiteboard, her classroom blurred behind her. A worker in waterproof coveralls folded his arms and dominated his picture's foreground, half obscuring a blunt little trawler.

But, when Harry examined the figures, other shapes emerged, or seemed to have emerged, unfolding in memory not sight. And he felt very strongly that each picture was several at once and that several of him looked on.

The teacher marked exercise books, and she held a hand that did not hold hers. There was a hospital bed and the hand she held felt dry and hot and limp, and she'd left her supper when the nurse called and said to her, 'I think it's time.' And the teacher was thinking, now, now, now, now, now. Please.

Vanessa returned. Her footsteps clacked and echoed. She handed him a glass. He sipped. The wine was sharp and crisp. He heard traffic beyond the room. A siren. And still, somewhere, he heard the teacher.

'Does your head in,' he said. 'How do you do it?'

She shrugged. 'I capture what I can. I look for layers.'

'Are you going to capture me?' He smiled slightly, and sipped his drink. The idea intrigued him, but he had no intention of standing still long enough to be caught by anyone.

She looked at him. Narrowed her eyes. Then she raised her eyebrows and inclined her head, indicating a patch of wall behind him. Just enough space for another canvas. 'Maybe,' she said. 'I was thinking of it. You sell things, right?'

'Not like him,' he nodded over at the businessman. An estate agent, he guessed. And then he knew. The man called his clients yourself, and bowed slightly when he met them. He wore patterned shirts and, one Wednesday afternoon, had sex with a potential customer in the back seat of his Mondeo. 'Now that's what I call a commission,' he said after he'd come on her blouse, not caring that he'd left her neither satisfied nor happy. She'd not been a serious prospect anyway.

'You don't sell things?' said Vanessa.

'I locate desire.' He waved at the estate agent. 'He wants status. The teacher wants love, comfort, and the world a better place. That sort of thing. It's easy to see because the research is out there. The categories tell you what people want. So I take it, the idea of it at least, and I bundle it up into badges and labels.'

He stepped closer to her. She swayed a little towards him. Just a dip.

'And what about you?' she said, 'What do you want?'

He shrugged and grinned. 'Right now?' He wondered where they might go. There was probably a couch somewhere. This was almost the moment. He could feel it.

'What do you want from your life, I mean.'

The question irritated him. People spent too much time worrying about their lives, and they were too easily satisfied with emotional cement, pre-chewed pap squeezed like paste into the gaps that opened up between themselves and their ideas of themselves. Lucky for him. Really there is only now. And not falling off the edge. Not ending up selling newspapers in a stupid hat, or calling some shift supervisor sir. You drive a nice car. And you know the secret. He wanted to undress her. He wanted to run his hand up underneath her skirt. He was very close now. He leaned in.

She lifted her arm and touched his cheek, checked his movement. 'You're sweet,' she said. Her pupils had dilated, he saw. Only thin bands of blue iris left.

He felt his breathing stop. Strangely it didn't panic him. He rocked. And sank. It was not a collapse. It was a folding. He was glad to feel the floor smooth and cool beneath his palms. It tilted.

*

'Think about your job,' she said. 'Start there.'

He thought of the Costello account, their diamond swoop logo, and how he'd made it ring. Effortless affluence for middle income strivers.

'We're aiming at people who want, John,' he had said to the MD. 'We want people who want to get beyond wanting, but never will. They're anxious and the Costello label will prove they're not.'

'Keep going,' said Vanessa. He could feel her hand now, cool on his forehead. As if he had a fever.

There was the day of the golf shoot, when he saw it would work. The grey eyes of the model, and the no-no-no-ing of the director. And Marianne, who managed the catering and wanted to change careers, she said. Sulky faced gofers, and the course manager hovering around the crew.

'It will be over by four, won't it? As agreed?'

And the diamond swoosh just everywhere, on the leather gloves, the sunglasses, discreetly badging the pastel sweater. The sun glinted on the model's watch. Harry felt certain then. It was a moment of security, of a life well navigated, a death distant, invisible, never coming.

And later, drunk, he had sex with Marianne in the closet office the course had let them use. Piles of manila folders. Old golfing magazines.

'That's right, what else?' said Vanessa. 'What else have you got for me?'

It was hurting now. Like peeling a scab and finding it unready to give. Arguing with Laura not about one anniversary but an anxious constellation of them. First date, first fuck, first holiday. And her friend Sandra who sulked in his presence and made clipped comments about patriarchy and told Laura he was a pig. He had put his hand on her arse, Sandra's that is, standing on the stair when she'd come up to use the bathroom after him. And she'd regarded him with such loathing. She hadn't had to slap him, or say a word. That look made her electric. He saw it wasn't a pose or a come-on. He saw he truly disgusted her.

And all along as this slid out of him, as she pulled it from him, he was thinking: some private view. Not the view I expected is it? Not my view. Her view. And he was almost grateful to be taken this way. It nauseated him, but that too he almost liked.

Vanessa pulled on. But nothing more came. It was like when lust dries up on you without warning, leaving sex a chore.

'There,' she said.

And she let the room back in. He was sitting on the floor with his legs stuck out straight. She crouched above him. He wondered confusedly if they'd just had sex. But they were both dressed. Very wide eyes, he thought. Set too far apart. In fact, there was something wrong about all her dimensions. Nothing you could prove. Her fingers. Very long fingers.

*

She led him to the front door.

He got as far as the top step then turned, intending to say something to punctuate the night. To make him feel less like he'd failed a test he hadn't even asked to take. But she had already shut him out.

He half expected to see her again. He drank in the nautical bar on Friday evenings. He began a half-hearted affair with an accountant who insulted him when she came. It turned out he liked that. The stark honesty of her contempt all tangled up in the lust. It made them sort of even.

One day, long after the exhibition had opened and the critics had finished with it, he went for a look. On his patch of wall, though, there was only a fire extinguisher and no painting. Nothing there at all.

Matt Zandstra was born in London and brought up in Belgium and the south-east of England. He graduated in 1990 from Sussex University with a 2:1 in Philosophy with Literature. He spent some years as an internet developer and worked most recently for Yahoo! in California. He returned to the UK to focus on writing in 2010.